SPECIAL MESSAGE TO READERS

This book is published under the auspices of

THE ULVERSCROFT FOUNDATION

(registered charity No. 264873 UK)

Established in 1972 to provide funds for research, diagnosis and treatment of eye diseases.

Examples of contributions made are: —

A Children's Assessment Unit at Moorfield's Hospital, London.

•

Twin operating theatres at the Western Ophthalmic Hospital, London.

•

A Chair of Ophthalmology at the Royal Australian College of Ophthalmologists.

•

The Ulverscroft Children's Eye Unit at the Great Ormond Street Hospital For Sick Children, London.

You can help further the work of the Foundation by making a donation or leaving a legacy. Every contribution, no matter how small, is received with gratitude. Please write for details to:

THE ULVERSCROFT FOUNDATION,
The Green, Bradgate Road, Anstey,
Leicester LE7 7FU, England.
Telephone: (0116) 236 4325

In Australia write to:

THE ULVERSCROFT FOUNDATION,
c/o The Royal Australian and New Zealand College of Ophthalmologists,
94-98 Chalmers Street, Surry Hills,
N.S.W. 2010, Australia

LOVE IS ALL AROUND

When Holly and Granny Jean embark on a round-Britain cruise, Holly little expects to meet up with Ben. Accompanying his grandad, he's wildly attractive, but annoyingly confident. However, after a bad start, Holly is drawn, irresistibly, to a more likeable side to Ben. But Grandad is grumpy, whilst Granny Jean is determinedly cheerful — and the entertainment hostess is more than a little interested in Ben. Holly is left wondering if this is good or bad!

Books by Beth James
in the Linford Romance Library:

IT STARTED WITH A KISS
UNBREAK MY HEART
THE SILVER VINAIGRETTE
OUT OF REACH
STRANGERS IN THE NIGHT
THE AUDACIOUS HIGHWAYMAN
TAKE MY BREATH AWAY

BETH JAMES

LOVE IS ALL AROUND

Complete and Unabridged

LINFORD
Leicester

First published in Great Britain in 2011

First Linford Edition
published 2012

British Library CIP Data

James, Beth.
Love is all around. - -
(Linford romance library)
1. Love stories.
2. Large type books.
I. Title II. Series
823.9′2–dc23

ISBN 978–1–4448–1181–0

Published by
F. A. Thorpe (Publishing)
Anstey, Leicestershire

Set by Words & Graphics Ltd.
Anstey, Leicestershire
Printed and bound in Great Britain by
T. J. International Ltd., Padstow, Cornwall

This book is printed on acid-free paper

1

'Exciting, isn't it?' her grandmother said, an excited light shining in her twinkling blue eyes.

Trying to ignore the fact that everyone in the queue ahead of her was at the very least twice her own age, Holly smiled broadly.

'I've never been on a cruise before either.'

'It'll be fun,' Granny Jean said. 'I have a feeling it's going to be one of the greatest experiences I've ever had.'

Hmm. Holly wasn't too sure about that. Already she had the feeling of being on a school trip, what with the queuing and things being explained in loud clear voices — often in triplicate.

She peered over the shoulder of the silver haired gentleman in front to see what the hold up was. Oh, they were taking official photos now, just before embarkation.

A querulous voice came from behind her.

'I don't know why we're having to wait so long . . . Don't they realise some of us are elderly?'

'I'm sure they do, Gramps,' came the rejoinder in a younger, light, masculine tone. 'It would be hard not to, with all these blue rinses and walking-sticks.'

'Well, Ben, you can't say I didn't warn you. It always was a damn fool idea, and what you're going to do with yourself for entertainment I can't imagine at all.'

'You don't have to, Gramps. Don't worry about me. Now, stop being such an old misery or I'll confiscate your walking stick and confine you to a wheelchair for the rest of the holiday.'

The older man gave a rasp which could have been an indicator of amusement or, more likely, just a clearing of the throat.

'Less of your impertinence, you

cheeky young puppy. You coerced me into this, you and your mother, ganging up on me the way you did, and you've got your own way. Well, I'm here — but you can't make me like it!' The old man's voice held a note almost of triumph.

There was a long drawn out sigh.

'Gramps, you're not listening. Mum said I was to stand no nonsense from you and I warn you, I won't! Now, start practising your smile for the camera before I dump you over the side!'

By this time Holly was dying to cast a casual glance over her shoulder in order to discover the appearance of the fellow travellers behind her.

Poor old guy. He sounded a bit down in the mouth, admittedly, but surely his grandson could show a little more patience and respect! That was his grandfather, after all.

Her gran gave a meaningful roll of her eyes.

'Happy holidays!' she said in Holly's ear.

Holly grinned and, adjusting the strap of her tote bag, gave a seemingly indifferent glance over her shoulder before the queue started moving again. As glances went, it was only fleeting, but still long enough for her to take in the two tall figures behind her.

The elder of the two had thinning hair and was slightly stooped, but the eyes that met hers for an instant, were sharp and full of life.

Holly gave a brief friendly smile, which was answered with a twitch of the lips so slight she thought afterwards it might have been imagined.

She hazarded a guess that his companion was thirty or thereabouts. He had dark, very thick hair, a tanned skin and eyes as equally bright as his grandfather's were.

Those eyes were looking at her now with an amused inspection, which she judged as too brazen and assessing by far.

Blushing slightly, she quickly turned away. Good, it was nearly their turn to be photographed; they'd soon be on board.

Taking care not to look his way again, Holly posed next to her granny for the photo that she guessed to be the first of many to be taken on the trip.

It was stupid to feel so self-conscious, standing waiting for the photographer to do his stuff. True, she'd never enjoyed having her picture taken but an audience of a grumpy old man and his too impertinent grandson was outside her experience and oddly disconcerting.

Oh, well, thank goodness it was done now.

She took her grandmother's arm and walked the remaining distance on to the ship. There was another small wait as an official card was handed out to each passenger.

'Always look on the bright side of life,' sang a voice behind her. Ben and his grandfather had obviously caught up again. Ignore him, Holly, she thought to herself.

Even though it's a big ship, he's

obviously a creep, and the last thing you want on this trip is to be entertaining a creep! She decided to avoid eye contact. After all, they hadn't been formally introduced, and there was no reason to be even remotely friendly.

* * *

Ben watched with undisguised admiration as Holly's shapely figure disappeared from view into the lift. Pretty girl, he thought. Actually, more than pretty. Sleek, conker-brown hair; warm, deep brown eyes. Reminded him of a song he couldn't quite think of at the moment, he only knew he'd like to see those eyes again.

Briefly, he wondered which floor — or rather, deck — her cabin would be situated on.

Not that knowing would help: she was probably sharing it with her aunt or her grandmother or whoever the elderly lady with her was.

With a shrug of his shoulders, he cast an eye over the other passengers immediately within his view. Not much talent here, then. Just as well, really. Distractions were not to be welcomed.

He needed whatever time he had left over from keeping an eye on Gramps to devote entirely to his project. He frowned a little, because he had to admit, even if only to himself, that his project at the moment was stuck fast with a dead body at the harbour-master's office in Ipswich.

Still, as most authors knew, a fresh scene, a new slant on life could work wonders for the creative juices, he decided. The trick was to start looking at this holiday as less of a penance, and more as an ideal opportunity to focus on his task.

'We don't need to take the lift, Ben,' Gramps said. 'I can manage the stairs if I take one step at a time. I'm perfectly capable . . .

'If only other people would stop pushing and shoving!' he added rather too loudly as a large lady, in a particularly violent-puce frock, threatened to knock him over from behind.

'Okay, we'll take the stairs,' Ben agreed, and started humming again.

* * *

Holly sat on her bed and examined the cabin she would be sharing with Granny Jean. It was small, but then, they were both small people. There was plenty of space in the wardrobe, three drawers each in the dressing-table between the comfortable beds, and a TV angled so they could both watch it comfortably. The bathroom cubicle was sparklingly clean and quite large enough, too.

'This is nice.' Granny Jean looked out of the porthole. 'A window, too. And just think — we got this at two-thirds of the price! What a lucky thing you saw the advert. I don't know what I've done to deserve such a lovely, thoughtful granddaughter.'

Holly laughed.

'I don't, either. It had nothing to do with the fact that I've always wanted to go to the Scottish islands and to Dublin. Nothing at all to do with the fact that I had holidays owing and nothing planned! Besides, strangely enough, I like spending time with you more than almost anything else in the world.'

Granny Jean put her head on one side and gazed at Holly out of bright, intelligent eyes. Holly looked back. Impossible to think that, only a month or so ago, her granny could barely see anything out of those eyes, she thought, swallowing. She'd promised herself that, if Granny Jean's eye operation went well, she would somehow manage to take her on the cruise around the islands of Britain that she'd talked about for so long. And here they were. The holiday included the Scottish islands, Dublin, The Channel Islands and Honfleur. How lucky, then, that once the doctor had said the operation was a success and her granny could travel, Holly had seen the advertised last-minute offer, which meant they could book up to join the cruiser at Harwich, only a stone's throw from their home town of Colchester. Yes, it was surely meant to be.

Remembering her excited reaction when she'd shown her the tickets and the brochure, she smiled now as Granny Jean gave her a quick hug.

'We'll have less of the flannel! But I want you to know I'm really very grateful, Holly. It's so nice to have someone to share this with.'

Holly hugged her back, then turned away, busying herself with unpacking her case.

'Now, we'll probably have a fire drill soon, and after that we can sit on deck and have some tea, and find out which table we've been allocated for dinner. We're on second sitting, at eight o'clock. That'll give us time to explore the ship and find out what else there is to do.'

'Yes,' Granny Jean agreed, who despite being seventy-five was always eager to find out what was going on.

'I'm dying to see the jacuzzi, I think it's on the top deck. I brought my cossy, it's pink with a halter neck. I hope it's not too young for me.'

'Impossible,' Holly said with a poker face.

* * *

It was no good, Ben thought. Sharing a cabin when both inhabitants were over six foot was a hazardous business. Although he was a neat, efficient man, well used to travel and economy packing, it soon became apparent that Gramps was not!

Of course, up until six months before, Ben's grandmother had always been around to do the packing, the organising and anything else it was felt that Gramps, being a mere man, was unable to deal with. Her sudden death had left poor old Gramps floundering in a sea of unexplained domesticity, which he found bewildering and deeply resented.

Ben understood all this, because his mother had explained it to him.

'But, Mum,' he'd argued. 'I can't believe a man of eighty is so incapable, and not only incapable, but also incredibly angry with anyone who dares to try to help him!'

'I know. Goodness knows, my patience is wearing thin. He's changed so much since Mum died . . . I don't know if this holiday will help or make things worse. It might be entirely the wrong thing to do! I only know we have to do something to bring him back from his unhappiness and also his deep hatred of himself.'

Ben had looked at his mother, usually so confident and so strong. Now she appeared tired and defeated.

She sighed.

'The trip was booked nearly a year ago. Somehow I've managed to persuade him to go on it, with you taking Mum's ticket. But I warn you, Ben, it won't be easy.'

'Don't worry, Mum, I'll sort him out.' Ben gave his most cocksure grin.

'Remember, he's still grieving. He'll never talk about it, but he is.'

'I know.'

Remembering this now, at the same time as watching Gramps trying to make the earth-shattering decision between putting his socks in the top drawer or the one beneath, Ben touched his arm.

'Let's leave this for now. We'll take a stroll round the ship and get our bearings. You'll be more successful at that than I will. Your spatial awareness has always been better than mine.'

Gramps straightened up with the beginnings of relief in his eyes. The side of his mouth twitched.

It was the closest thing on his grandfather's lips to a smile Ben had seen for some time now.

'Spatial awareness,' he repeated. 'In my day they called it 'finding your way around'. Hmm . . . spatial awareness, indeed.'

'Come on, Gramps. Let's put you to the test and see which of us can find the bar first!'

* * *

The Anastasia set sail promptly at six. The sea was calm, and the evening sunlight bathed the deck where Holly and her gran were sitting. The next couple of hours passed very agreeably. Granny Jean struck up conversations with at least three different couples, all the while exclaiming over the smoothness of the sea, the friendliness of the staff and how much she was looking forward to seeing Tobermory and the other Scottish islands, not to mention the rest of the trip.

When Holly judged Granny Jean to be talked out, for the moment at least, she suggested they went back to their cabin for a rest before changing for dinner. It was casual dress for dinner that evening. Holly chose a pretty summer skirt and a top printed with amber and brown, which suited her colouring, she knew.

Granny Jean was wearing a grey dress with a soft pink pashmina draped around her shoulders. With her silver hair smartly cut into a bob, her bright enquiring manner and her upright stance, Holly felt very proud indeed to be her granddaughter.

'You look the business!' she said.

The old lady chuckled.

'I must remember that. 'The business', eh? That sounds modern.'

They left their cabin at the same time as the couple next door. Granny Jean was as politely inquisitive as usual. By the time they had all negotiated the stairs and found the entrance to the restaurant, she had exchanged names, discussed how lovely the ship was, what a packed and exciting itinerary they appeared to have ahead of them, and the fact that the other couple also had a granddaughter who was studying at Leeds university.

Holly listened in dumbfounded admiration. Granny Jean, who had only ever been a housewife, possessed more people skills in her little finger than any of the personal relations officers that Holly had ever come across had learned in the whole of their careers!

The dining-room was beautifully laid out with gleaming cutlery and glasses, snowy-white table linen and a row of smartly dressed, smiling staff ready to welcome them positioned just inside the doors. Together Holly and Granny Jean bade a temporary goodbye to their neighbours, wished them a good evening and followed the waiter to their designated table of eight.

'How lovely,' her grandmother murmured. 'I do love a round table. So much more friendly.'

Holly's answering comment died on her lips, for sitting next to the two spaces indicated by the waiter, smiling invitingly and patting the empty seat next to him, was the tall, dark, granddad-threatening man who'd stood behind them in the embarkation queue.

2

'Let's hope that pathetic old relic will be a tad more agreeable tonight than last night.' Granny Jean fastened a silver necklace round her neck.

Holly looked up in surprise.

'Oh, he wasn't so bad as all that, Granny' she said sternly. 'Not all septuagenarians are as fit and lively as you're fortunate enough to be. And actually, he's nearly eighty.'

'How do you know that?'

'His grandson told me. Also, he's only recently been widowed. I'd have thought you'd be more tolerant.'

Granny Jean gave a small snort.

'I recognise the type,' she said shortly. 'He's feeling too sorry for himself to notice anything else going on around him. I bet he's never thanked that good-looking grandson of his for giving up a week of his life to come away with him. Probably never never given it a thought!'

'Ben told me the holiday had been booked for nearly a year, and his granddad had forgotten all about it. When he asked Ben's mum to cancel it, since obviously now his wife had died he didn't want to go, Ben suggested that he went with him instead.

'I think he considered it a waste not to use it, plus I don't think it's any great sacrifice on Ben's part. He probably regards it as a free holiday! He's a pretty heartless character, if you ask me. He actually said he's only here for the beer, and that if Gramps, is determined to be miserable, there's nothing much he can do about it.'

There was a pause.

'Anyway, he's not all that good-looking.'

'More than passable, I would say.' Granny Jean was looking at her slyly. 'And no doubt about it, Gramps — hmm — 'Grumps' would be more like it — does indulge in self-pity. It's no good doing that, it gets you nowhere.'

'Have a heart, Granny, the poor old guy is still suffering from shock. His wife only died seven months ago.'

'Tch. His soup was cold, the bread had too many seeds in it; he couldn't understand the waiter . . . honestly! No, Holly, when you're suddenly widowed you have to begin as you mean to go on. If you start by grumbling about everything, and being rude to everyone you meet, you're unlikely to suddenly have a change of heart just because a bit of time has gone past.'

Holly zipped herself into her tight black pants and shrugged on a silky, cream shirt, then added a sequinned waistcoat.

'There, d'you think I'm formal enough for a 'formal' evening? Not too Hallowe'en, is it?'

'You look gorgeous.' Granny Jean patted a stray hair into place. 'I wonder why they put us on the same table as Ben and his grandfather — what was his name again?'

'Roger, I think — no, it was Ron. Maybe it was because Ben and I are the only ones accompanying grandparents. There seem to be quite a few mothers and daughters on this trip, or families with grandparents, so they probably sort out likely combinations from the booking forms.'

'Maybe, but, if Ron booked this when his wife was still alive they wouldn't have known, would they?'

'Well, they have put us on the same table, and that's all there is to it. I can get it changed if you like, although all the others on our table are nice normal couples. If Ron is a bit awkward, well, I'm sure we can put up with it for a while.'

'Oh, darling.' Granny Jean was immediately contrite. 'Of course I don't want to change tables! I'm not complaining, really I'm not. It just seems such a waste to me when someone is so intent on being miserable. Quite a handsome fellow as well, for his age . . . if only he smiled a bit more!'

Holly grinned.

She almost could almost guarantee that, before the end of the week, old Ron would be standing up a little straighter and frowning a little less. That was the effect Granny Jean had on people!

* * *

'You'll have them running after you in droves, Gramps.'

Ignoring his grandson's flippant remark, Ron finished tying his bow tie and straightened up from the mirror, which was just a little too short for a man of his height.

'Made for the vertically challenged,' he muttered. 'I don't know why we have to get dressed up like this.'

Since, secretly, he was inclined to agree, Ben let that one go.

'Now, start thinking charming conversation, Gramps. It's time to be sociable.'

'I've been sociable all day,' Ron said wearily.

'Well, if you can really call attending a quiz — which we did really badly at, by the way — drinking coffee on the top deck, listening to a very pretty girl playing the violin and an equally pretty girl singing the classics, then falling asleep for two hours while I slaved away over my laptop socialising, then I suppose you have!

'But tonight, on our dinner-table, I expect more from you than the few grunts you treated us to last night.'

Ron bristled with indignation.

'I talked to Holly! Pretty little thing, I thought.'

'Correction, Gramps. She talked, you listened. It was mostly about the weather, I seem to recall. Oh, and the bread having too many seeds. And try to smile now and then, eh? It doesn't hurt, honestly! This might be torture for you, but the others on the table are here to enjoy themselves.

'That's better,' he went on as Gramps gave an unexpected baring of his teeth. 'Although you might modify it a little if you don't want to terrify the waiter tonight!'

He picked up the next day's itinerary,

which had been posted under their cabin door.

'We'll be in Invergorden tomorrow. How would you like a bus trip along the shore line of Loch Ness to Inverness? That could be quite interesting.' He folded the sheet of paper and put it in his jacket pocket.

Ron nodded a brief assent and looked round for his walking stick.

'Don't make me sit next to that Jean woman again, will you?'

Ben's eyebrows rose and he regarded his grandfather keenly.

'Why ever not?'

Gramps glanced away.

'I don't know. She makes me feel inadequate. I haven't a clue what to talk to her about, and she, on the other hand, seems to have too much to say! Then anything I do say comes out all wrong, and I sound as though I'm moaning again.'

He wedged his fingers inside his collar as though to ease it, although as far as Ben could see it was far from tight. Suddenly, for all his height, his grandfather, dressed in his too-big shirt and wearing an expression close to terror, looked very frail and vulnerable.

'Come on, Gramps, we're doing fine.' He passed the old man's walking-stick to him. 'I'll make sure you don't sit near Jean if she makes you uncomfortable. All you have to do is eat your dinner and be nice.'

And that's all I have to do, as well, Ben thought to himself. No need to be annoyed because Holly, the girl with the brown eyes, never looked in his direction if she could possibly help it.

No earthly point in feeling somewhat put out because she laughed at everyone else's jokes but not at his. No reason to feel upset because, although she'd sat next to him at dinner last night, he'd had the feeling it was only because she had no choice, and that actually it was the last thing in the world she wanted to do.

What had he done, he wondered, to cause such antipathy? He'd had a shower and cleaned his teeth, hadn't he? He hadn't told any rude jokes, made indecent proposals or slurped his soup. He'd made polite conversation, or rather tried to, but she'd frozen him out, seeming to prefer Gramps to him, although she had seemed sympathetic when Ben had confided the background to the trip.

Why didn't she like him? Ben Brown, the closest, probably the only, unattached male passenger on board to be anywhere near her own age! Why did she so obviously hold him in aversion?

He wasn't used to being disliked. Forgetting his earlier resolution that this was to be a working holiday — just him and his laptop from two till six each day, working on his project while Gramps rested — he decided he would change Holly's mind. That, before the holiday was finished, he'd have her eating out of his hand.

Ben Brown was used to getting what he wanted, and the truth was he liked having a girlfriend. It didn't have to be a serious relationship, with all the accompanying connotations. He was quite happy with casual, flirty affairs. Superficial, perhaps, but relationships that were easy, didn't take up too much time.

Fun relationships, not to be regarded too deeply by either party, with no strings at all.

He enjoyed being funny, charming, interesting and attentive — oh, yes, he could do them all. Smart, sassy women appealed to him, but he also appreciated a bit of a challenge.

He particularly liked it when they looked at him as though they thought they knew exactly what he was all about. As though his charm was only skin deep and they could puncture his confidence at a stroke. Invariably they were always unprepared for his counter attack, which was his ability to laugh at himself.

That, and his very genuine interest in what made them laugh, what made them cry and what they were all about.

Even now, Ben's eyes searched for

Holly as he walked behind his grandfather into the dining room. Ah, there she was, and she looked . . . well, she looked stunning.

Ben smiled into her eyes.

'You look amazing.'

Holly had been listening to a conversation between another couple, Linda and Tony, and Granny Jean, so she just laughed nervously and focused on Ben's bow tie. Why was it that women spent hours titivating and agonising over what to wear, whereas a man had only to don a fresh white shirt and an evening suit to look completely devastating?

But she was not about to be taken in. This Ben character was too full of himself by far; she'd met the type before. They thought they only had to smile at a woman for her to be putty in their hands.

Well, not so. Not in Holly's case.

'Amazing', for goodness sake. 'Smart', would have been good enough. 'Lovely' a little too much. 'Great', completely acceptable. But amazing? In her experience amazing meant phenomenal, astounding, both things that Holly had no wish to be. Yes, she had been right about Ben; he was a little too full of charm and easy compliments to be true.

Lucky, then, that tonight she didn't have to sit next to him, but was instead seated between Granny Jean and Tony the ex-policeman, who proved to be quite jolly and easy to talk too. Holly smiled politely at a comment he'd just made and, trying not to notice Ben at the other side of the table who was flirting outrageously with the pretty wine waitress, tucked into her seeded roll and butter.

Once again, the dinner they were served proved to be enjoyable. Gramps refrained from passing comment on the rolls, and apparently the soup was served at the exact temperature he liked. Holly could see he was making an effort. Linda and Tony were good company, and dinner gradually drew out to be a sociable and lengthy occasion.

'Oh, if we're not careful we'll miss

'Showtime'!' Granny Jean glanced at her watch in consternation.

Holly quickly finished her coffee and took her grandmother's arm.

'We didn't go yesterday.' Ron reached for his walking-stick. 'Was it worth seeing?'

'Worth seeing?' Granny Jean echoed. 'Of course it was worth seeing. If you don't see it, how can you know what you're missing? The dancers are very talented and the singers really professional.'

A flush came to Ron's face.

'Not the sort of thing I usually go in for,' he muttered.

As they trooped out of the restaurant and down towards the other end of the ship Holly found that, somehow, she was walking next to Ben.

'I'm sorry about Granny Jean's comments to your grandad,' she found herself saying. 'I don't know what's come over her, she's not usually so sharp-tongued.'

'Don't worry about it. She's doing

him the world of good. At least he's noticing what's going on now. Before he came on board he swore he wouldn't go to any of their 'damn silly shows', and now here he is, following your Granny like a lamb to the slaughter!'

Holly chuckled.

'Oh, she won't actually kill him. She draws the line at bloodshed. Ah, here we are. Shh, it's started.'

Sure enough, the lights were dim, and a very pretty Eastern European girl was singing a well-known ballad. Ben led the way to three empty seats at the very back of the auditorium, and motioned them to sit down. It wasn't long before he'd procured them all drinks and took his own place on a bar stool behind them.

Grateful that there was no way Ben could carry on even a whispered conversation from two foot above and behind her, Holly watched the show, which was fast-paced and colourful.

When, some hours later, the show ended, she joined in the applause appreciatively. She was surprised when Ben whistled and called for an encore. Somehow it didn't seem like the kind of thing he would do.

'The bar at the other end of the ship is still open, if you fancy a nightcap, Gramps,' he said. 'There's still some music going on down there.'

'No, I think I'll turn in,' Ron said.

'Right. I'll be along later. Ben turned, raised his eyebrows and looked at Holly in invitation.

She opened her mouth to decline, then looked at Granny Jean.

'What an excellent idea,' the old lady said. 'If you go along with Ben, it'll give me time to get to bed before you. There's not much room in those cabins. I could do with a bit of privacy!'

Anything she said now would be bound to come across as nothing less than rude. Glaring at her granny, Holly shut her mouth again.

'Now, if you'll just point me in the right direction for our cabin . . . ' Granny Jean said.

'I'd better take you back as far as the lift, in case you get lost,' Holly offered hopefully.

'Hmm. I'm rather hoping Gramps will — get lost, I mean,' Ben watched as Ron made his way confidently, if slowly, down the passageway. 'But no such luck, he's a navigator extroadinaire!'

After depositing Granny Jean in the lift, with instructions to keep to the corridor on the left when she reached the right deck, Holly and Ben made their way towards the other end of the ship.

The atmosphere in the bar was relaxed. The lights were dim, one of the good-looking entertainment hosts was crooning softly into the microphone and several couples were dancing.

Ben slid himself onto a bench seat. Holly sat in a bucket-shaped seat about a foot away. Immediately a waitress appeared alongside them. Ben ordered a beer and asked Holly what she'd like.

'A coffee would be nice.'

'Not much fun to be had from a coffee.'

'Fun is not something I particularly crave.'

'That's a shame. You have a look about you that's made for fun, I would have to say.'

'I don't recall asking you.'

The song finished and there was a thin smattering of applause. Feeling slightly ashamed of herself for her last remark Holly joined in.

'So, what made you decide to come on this trip?' Ben asked as though the previous exchange had never taken place.

'My grandmother has just recovered from an eye operation. I knew she'd often looked at this particular trip and said she'd like to do it. As luck would have it, there was a special deal going and I had some time owing. Besides, Granny Jean practically brought me up. I enjoy spending time with her.' She paused. 'How about you?'

'Much the same thing. Oh, we didn't get a special deal or anything. But as I told you, the cruise was booked already, then Grandma died and well, poor old Gramps has lost the will to enjoy himself.' He shrugged and adopted a phony American accent. 'My mission on this voyage is to try and help him find it again.'

'It's early days,' Holly ventured after a pause in which she registered that, clearly, Ben did care at least a little about his grandfather.

'Yes, but he is nearly eighty, and at the moment he just can't be bothered to do anything. Won't go to the doctor, won't entertain counselling, just shuts himself up in his house and does nothing. Not even the crossword puzzle, which he used to take pride in finishing before lunch. My mother went round the other day at three o'clock in the afternoon and he was still in his pyjamas.'

'Oh, dear.'

'Yes,' Ben agreed. 'Definitely oh, dear! His brain's sharp enough, but my fear is that, if he doesn't start using it again soon, he'll just sink further and further into melancholy.' He looked away. 'If I can just get him to join in a little, take an interest in life again.'

'He seemed to enjoy the show tonight,' Holly offered.

'Did he? I couldn't see from where I was sitting.'

'When you whistled and called out, I thought I saw him give a grin.'

'Good. Now, what do I have to do to have the same effect on you?' He raised his eyebrows comically.

'Nothing.' Holly accepted her coffee, which had just arrived. 'I can grin quite easily, entirely unaided!'

A more lively piece of music was being performed now, and for a moment they sat quietly sipping at their drinks. Suddenly Holly found that she wasn't in quite such a hurry to end the evening. Another modicum of clapping, and a different singer took her place on the small podium.

'I'd ask you to dance if I thought there was the remotest chance you'd say yes.'

Carefully, Holly replaced her coffee cup into its saucer.

'Your instincts are good.'

'Ah!' He looked self-satisfied.

'What do you mean — ah?' she countered, irked by the man's smugness.

'Long-standing boyfriend at home. It's written all over you.'

Holly clicked her tongue impatiently.

'The conceit of the male species never ceases to surprise me! No, I don't have a long standing boyfriend at home. Perhaps the notion that I might not want to dance with you never entered your head as a possibility?'

Ben's eyes crinkled at the corners.

'Sorry,' he said. 'I suppose I asked for that.' His smile broadened. 'Some girls don't dance on the first date.'

'And some girls don't dance, full stop. Anyway, this is not a first date.'

'Of course not. But you must agree, the average age on this cruise is a little daunting.'

'Not for me,' Holly replied. Then,

because she was curious, 'How old are you exactly?'

'Twenty-nine, the best age to be. Readily available to all females aged eighteen to forty!'

She stared at him. He hadn't really said that, had he?

'You need advice on your chat-up lines,' she said frostily. 'That came across as totally and completely obnoxious.'

Smiling, as though he was enjoying himself hugely, Ben leaned back in his seat.

'I think you're overstating the case. Totally and completely mean the same thing — surely?'

Holly picked up her bag.

'I'm really tired. Thanks for the coffee. Goodnight.'

'I'll see you in the morning.'

'Not if I see you first,' Holly said to the swing door as she left the bar.

3

For some strange reason Holly woke up in a disagreeable mood. The Anastasia had docked in the early hours, but outside the air looked to be misty and uninviting.

'I expect it will soon clear,' Granny said. 'We're at Invergordon. The gateway to the Scottish Highlands — doesn't that sound romantic?'

'Doesn't look too seeped in romance to me.' Holly raised a tousled head from her pillow.

'We're not on an excursion today, are we?'

'No, it was the castles, and we decided we'd rather be independent and take a bus along the shore of Loch Ness, and visit Inverness.'

Holly could never stay in a cross mood for long, so, ignoring the feeling that she'd overreacted to Ben's stupid comments of the previous night, she forced herself to smile her way through breakfast. Nevertheless, she gave a sigh of relief when she didn't spot either Ron or Ben. Not that she'd been looking for them, of course.

They almost missed the large double-decker bus into Inverness, but by the time they both scrambled on board a watery sun was attempting a tentative appearance.

'Sorry, Granny,' Holly said when informed that the upper deck was full, 'If I'd been a bit quicker we would have got a seat on top and had a better view of the loch. Who knows, we might have spotted the monster!'

'This is fine.' Her granny settled herself in a seat halfway along the lower deck. 'Bus steps are a bit steep for me. I wasn't really expecting to see Nessie, but did you know that the Loch Ness monster was first mentioned in a chronicle in the sixth century AD?'

Holly's eyebrows rose a fraction.

'Oh, come on Granny, where did you

get that piece of information from?'

'The television,' Granny Jean answered smugly.

* * *

'The river Ness,' Ben informed a granite-faced Gramps sitting next to him on the top deck, 'runs through the centre of Inverness, presenting a picturesque riverside walk. It's crossed in several places by charming bridges. In the seventeenth century the Brahan Seer (known to be gifted with the second sight) prophesied that, when seven bridges crossed the Ness, there would be a catastrophe in the town.'

'Yes?' Gramps said with heavy sarcasm. 'And what happened? Did Nessie come and eat them all up?'

'No.' Ben's eyes gleamed triumphantly. 'But in nineteen eighty-nine, shortly after the seventh bridge was built, a railway bridge collapsed!'

'Well?' his grandfather urged.

'That's it.'

'Poppycock. Hardly a catastrophe.'

'If you were standing on the bridge at the time you might not say that.'

'Hmm! What else has Inverness to offer?'

'Tartans and tweeds; gift shops selling Celtic jewellery . . . The castle isn't open to the public. Lots of interesting walks, though.'

'Right,' Gramps muttered unenthusiastically.

Ben shot him a despairing look, and closed his guide book. There was a steady hum of voices from the rest of the passengers on the bus but it seemed that, today, Gramps had decided to be even less communicative than usual.

Right, so be it. Trying for a more comfortable position for his long legs, Ben hunkered down in his seat and gave himself up to his own thoughts. After Holly had left him at the bar last evening, he had ordered another drink and silently berated himself for being every kind of fool. Why on earth had he let his clever tongue run away with him?

All very well, these imaginary conversations invented to make him seem witty and sharp. Not quite so impressive when practised in real life, in an effort to impress a pretty girl! What had got into him? He knew that in the company of other girls he'd never come out with anything so crass.

He scowled to himself. Somehow, he'd allowed Holly, with her fresh-faced prettiness, beautiful brown eyes and kind nature to get under his skin. But this morning he reflected maybe Holly wasn't quite such a sweet girl after all. A couple of her comments last night had been uncalled for, surely?

She'd needled him, goaded him into showing his worst side. Of course he didn't think he was God's gift to all women aged between eighteen and forty! How could she have possibly thought he was serious?

But anyway, why should he care what she thought?

His evening had ended quite abruptly and earlier than he'd intended when one of the ship's entertainment hostesses had come purposefully towards him. At any other time, Ben would have leaped to his feet and invited her to dance, but somehow a smooch with the attractive, heavily made-up blonde held little appeal. He'd avoided her eye and stood up to finish his drink, giving her a rueful smile over his shoulder as he left.

That same entertainment hostess was on the bus this morning. He'd spotted her in the queue, just as Gramps was observing that he hadn't stood in a bus queue for near on thirty years. She'd opened her mouth to speak to them both, but luckily someone else had grabbed her attention and asked how long it would take to get to Inverness.

It transpired that the journey took about forty minutes, and by the time they arrived the weather was brightening up. Ben only wished the same could be said for Gramps's frame of mind.

* * *

'Shall we stop here for a coffee?'

After visiting the Victorian Market, Holly and and her grandmother had spent a pleasant hour or so browsing the shops in the High Street that led down towards Ness Bridge. Granny Jean had bought postcards and a tea-towel, heavily embellished with pictures of heather and tartan.

'I know not so many people use tea-towels these days, but they're always an acceptable gift and it's a little reminder of our holiday.'

The Celtic jewellery had tempted Holly, and she'd allowed her grandmother to buy her a silver pendant of modern Celtic design. The self-service coffee shop was crowded.

'You find a seat,' Holly suggested. 'I'll get the coffee. Do you want anything to eat?'

'What, after that enormous breakfast? I don't think so.'

Holly took her place in the queue which seemed to be moving remarkably slowly, but when she'd finally been served and turned, tray in hands, to look for her grandmother she was met with the unwelcome sight of Granny's sleek silver head close to a head of thick, dark hair that she recognised only too easily.

Well, there was nothing else for it, plastering a smile of surprise on her face she went across to join them.

Ben acknowledged her with a lift of an eyebrow.

'Where's your grandad?' Holly asked.

'At Jean's inspired suggestion, he's hot-footing it back to the gift shop to buy my mother a tea-towel. It's not much, I'll admit, but it's a start. I'm hoping he can rev himself up to buy her something a little more personal at a later stage, as a thank you for all she's had to put up with!'

'Apparently, his knee's playing up and he's thinking of going back to the ship,' Granny Jean volunteered. 'I must admit I'm feeling a little tired myself. This hill is quite steep. If I could trust myself to find my way back to the bus stop, I'd probably bow out of that riverside walk you wanted to take, Holly.'

'No problem, Gran. I'll take you back to the bus stop, and do the walk on my own.'

Ben took a last sip of his coffee, and looked up as his plastic-bag clutching grandfather came into view.

'Hi, Gramps. Well done, Mum'll love that!'

'Hmm. I am capable, you know, of making a purchase alone and unaided.' He wore a pained look.

'Of course you are,' Holly chimed in.

'Holly,' Ben said, looking at Gramps with an innocent smile, 'I'm sure Gramps would be delighted to escort your gran to the bus stop and the ship, and then we would both be left to do our own thing.'

Noticing that poor old Ron looked far from delighted, Holly felt her eyes narrow in suspicion.

'Excellent,' Granny Jean said. 'And you needn't look so frightened, Ron

— I won't be a bother. In fact, I'm so tired I'll probably have a snooze on the bus, so you won't even have to talk to me!

'After all,' she added persuasively, 'a couple of old crocks like us don't want to spoil the young peoples' fun, do we?'

The expression on Ron's face said that he wouldn't care about spoiling their fun — in fact, he might actually enjoy it.

But he replied that, of course, he would be delighted to escort her back on board.

'That's settled, then.' Ben had the expression of a Cheshire cat.

They stood together, watching as their two grandparents walked up the street together. Gramps leaned heavily, if somewhat theatrically, on his stick while Granny Jean, despite her earlier promise, was already talking nineteen to the dozen.

'That was adroitly done,' Holly said dryly.

'I thought so.'

'Well, you needn't look so smug.'

'I'll try not to. But the whole object of this exercise is to bring Gramps back to civilisation, and they don't come much more civilised than Granny.'

'She's not your granny,' said Holly petulantly.

'Okay, Jean. Is that better?'

They stood staring at each other for a moment, brown eyes looking into light ones that bore an annoying twinkle.

'Well, I'm off for my walk now,' Holly said eventually.

'Right,' Ben said, falling into step beside her.

'And where d'you think you're going?'

'A riverside walk, as recommended in the brochure. Been looking forward to it all morning, actually.'

'So have I — but I planned to do it alone.'

'No problem. Two sides to the riverbank, and paths along both of them. You choose your side, so that you can contemplate nature in peaceful solitude, and I'll do the other. Wouldn't dream of disturbing you.'

'Fine by me.'

Trying to swallow down the feeling that she was being ridiculous she strode on down the hill.

But Holly found she couldn't stay cross for long. Bright rays of sunshine slanted through the graceful, fresh green trees, which shaded the river walk. The water gurgled along beside her and the air was full of bird song. Perhaps she glanced across at the other bank rather more often than she would normally have done, registering that the tall, dark-haired figure on the opposite bank was walking slower than she would expect.

She gave herself a mental shake, annoyed that she was allowing that figure to infringe so much on her thoughts. But she was still enjoying herself, wasn't she?

She'd chosen the path at the far side of the bridge, and sauntered along at a leisurely pace, occasionally passing a walker coming from the other direction who she thought she recognised from The Anastasia. Yes, it was all very peaceful, very pleasant indeed. It was nice to have some time alone. Where else, she asked herself, would you feel as though you were in the middle of the countryside, when actually you were in the centre of a city?

Presently, she came to the Ness Islands bridge. It was made up of two small, narrow islands and then two even tinier ones, linked by a series of small quaint bridges. It was like something out of a fairy tale, and Holly caught her breath as, despite her resolve to stay on her side of the river she felt compelled to step on to the first bridge. The clear water swirled beneath her as she trod firmly over the bridge onto the first island.

It was so pretty. The sun had peeped out again from its short-lived disappearance behind a cloud, and fairly danced across the river that was cascading its way between and over the brown stones and rocks making up the river bed.

Were there any fish? she wondered, ducking under a tree branch to obtain a closer viewpoint. She couldn't see any, and wondered if perhaps the water was too acidic.

'Careful you don't fall in.'

Holly looked over her shoulder. Sure enough, sitting on a bench placed to incorporate the enchanting view, grinning annoyingly, was Ben.

'It's beautiful, isn't it?'

After a moment in which she contemplated ignoring him, she nodded.

'It's so clear and unpolluted, but there don't seem to be any fish in here.'

'Well, that fisherman over there obviously thinks there are.'

Despite herself Holly gave a laugh.

'Oh, yes. I didn't notice him . . . It's all so perfect, he just blends in with the surroundings, like part of a watercolour or something!'

Ben took his camera out.

'Would you mind if I took your

photo? The scenery's beautiful, but I'd like a figure on the bridge to show the scale of it.'

Holly opened her mouth to refuse, then closed it again. Half leaning on the bridge, she turned and smiled.

* * *

So, after all, it was as easy as that, Ben reflected later when they were back on the ship and had joined forces again together with the grandparents and the policeman and his wife as a quiz team. Suddenly, Holly had turned into someone friendly.

They'd arrived back in board almost too late for lunch. On spotting them, Granny Jean, who was just about to leave the buffet restaurant, stayed to have a second coffee with them.

She explained that she had linked up with another lady sitting alone, and they'd had a long conversation about hip replacements and eye operations.

'Over lunch?'

'Of course, over lunch,' Granny Jean replied. 'You get less squeamish as you get older. I don't know what's happened to Ron, I haven't seen him since we got back. He said he might look in on the quiz. It starts in fifteen minutes. I told him I'm hopeless at quiz questions.'

That, Ben realised later once the quiz was underway, was not strictly true. But it was enough to put a small smirk on Gramps's face as he answered one question after the other with a minimum of hesitation.

'My goodness!' Holly said with open admiration. 'However do you know all these things?'

'Always had a retentive memory,' Ron answered modestly. 'It's a gift.'

The next question proved to be about an actress from a popular soap. Granny Jean brightened.

'I know that one!' she said loudly before saying the answer in an equally loud voice.

'You don't have to shout it so loudly,'

Ron scolded. ‘Everyone will hear.’

‘It’s only a game, Ron,’ Granny Jean said, just beating Ben to it.

Holly and Ben exchanged looks, and she smiled.

Glory be, he thought. She likes me. This girl is really beginning to like me!

4

The next morning found the Anastasia docked at Stornoway, which was somewhere that Holly had never heard of, and a place that Granny Jean only remembered from shipping forecasts on the radio in the war years. The organised trip they planned to take today incorporated the Islands of Lewis and Harris. These, they learned, were the largest of the Western Isles, otherwise known as the Outer Hebrides.

'Maybe that's where Mendlesson wrote The Hebrides Overture,' Granny speculated. 'I know it was up here somewhere.'

'You'll have to ask Ron when you see him.'

Granny Jean chuckled.

'Yes, I think that man considers himself the fount of all knowledge after yesterday! There's another quiz late this afternoon, so he will no doubt get another chance to shine!'

Holly raised her eyebrows.

'Are you sure you want to repeat the experience?'

'Well, if there's nothing else on, and I don't feel too tired, I might.'

Her eyes crinkled at the corners.

'I rather enjoy annoying Ron — he takes it so seriously. He was cross, wasn't he, when we only came second instead of first?'

'You're a wicked old woman.'

'I know. But his being annoyed is an improvement on being apathetic, and that was what Ben described him as being before he came on this cruise. I rather like Ben.'

'So you keep saying.'

'Well? Don't you like him?'

'He's all right. A bit too know it all.'

'That seems to run in the family.'

'A bit selfish, too. He doesn't consider other people's feelings; too quick with the clever remarks, if you ask me.'

'Young men are notoriously shy of showing the caring, more feminine side of their natures.'

Holly choked on her breakfast tea.

'You've got to be kidding! There is no 'caring' side to him, and as for feminine, forget it!'

'You know what I mean. Anyway, he has kind eyes.'

'Kind eyes? They didn't look very kind when Gramps accidentally tripped him up with his walking-stick, I can tell you!'

Pausing as she was about to take a bite of toast, Granny Jean fixed Holly with one of her most bird-like stares.

'Are you sure that was an accident?'

Holly looked shocked.

'Of course it was an accident. Ron would be unlikely to deliberately trip up his own grandson!'

'Hmm,' Granny Jean said.

* * *

The trip to the isles of Lewis and Harris, often referred to as the twin isles as a mountainous border divides the two, proved to be bleak and cold but very interesting.

'I didn't realise my forebears, the Mackenzies, were such a war-like crowd,' Granny Jean remarked after listening, wide-eyed, to stories of bloody skirmishes between the Mackenzies and the equally fierce Macleods.

'I should have guessed it,' her granddaughter replied. 'You scare me!'

They visited the 2000-year-old broch at Carloway, a ruined defence made of grim-looking stone with the remains of an old stairway built within one of the walls.

Holly shivered.

'Your ancestors must have been tough . . . and agile,' she added, ducking to avoid a low piece of rock-like ceiling.

'They're your ancestors too, don't forget. You can be tough when the occasion calls for it. Poor Ben, you've hardly spoken to him all day.'

Holly was stung.

'There's no call for me to keep seeking him out to speak to him! I see enough at him at the dinner-table, thank you very much.'

As if to belie her words, within five minutes Holly missed her footing as she descended the incline leading down from the broch to the path.

'Whoa there!'

She was steadied by a strong hand, grasping her elbow. It felt as though some strange kind of electrical charge had shot right up her arm and into her . . . no, that was ridiculous. Her heart didn't come into this.

Holly looked up into a gaze so intense that it made her feel quite dizzy. She gave herself a shake.

'Thank you Ben.'

'Take more water with it next time,' he said with a grin.

'I will.' Holly was aware that he was still holding her closely, and that her heart wouldn't behave itself until he stopped holding her in quite that way. 'You can let go of me now.'

'Spoil sport.'

Flustered, she looked ahead for Granny, only to find her watching them over her shoulder with an 'I told you so' expression on her face.

'And there's no need to look at me like that,' Holly said when she caught up with her.

'Like what? I was just surprised to see you throwing yourself at him, that's all.'

'I was not throwing myself at him! I don't even like him, and you know it.' Holly wished her face was less fiery, and was annoyed by how shaken from his touch she still felt

'So you say . . . ' came Jean's response.

The next stop was the Gearrannan Blackhouse village. They all crowded together in the subdued light inside one of the small blackhouse dwellings. The blackhouses were made of stone with thatched roofs. Apparently, a newly married couple would be delighted to receive wooden rafters as wedding gifts as, with no trees growing on the island, wood was hard to come by.

The light inside was dim and the smell of burning peat pervaded the air. It was explained by their guide that the fumes from the peat fire escaped through the thatched roof, but that it also held antiseptic properties which made it a healthy atmosphere rather than detrimental in any way.

'No chimney, then?' Granny Jean asked.

'Not necessary.' Ron was standing close by.

'I wonder what their life expectancy was?'

Pretty good, actually,' Ben put in. 'As old as Gramps here — sometimes older! No stress, you see. They just tended their sheep, cut the peat, caught their fish, farmed their oats and told stories round their firesides. A simple life — a community life.'

'Yes, when they weren't planning how to kill each other,' Ron added in a sarcastic tone.

'They didn't kill each other all the time, Ron,' Granny Jean's voice was conciliating. 'They must have mostly lived together in harmony, surely.'

Her voice was wistful.

'With the elements to fight against, they must have looked out for one another. If they survived childhood, the people here were probably a healthy lot. There were few mental health issues, I should think, and very little actual loneliness there.'

Ron gave a twisted smile.

'Oh, I'm sure you're right, it was all a bed of roses.'

Abruptly, he turned away, but not before Holly had caught a glimpse of the aching isolation in his expression.

'Oh, dear, I said the wrong thing, didn't I?' Granny Jean said when they were safely on the coach again and out of earshot of Ron and his grandson, who were seated at the far end.

'He's still feeling a bit raw, I expect. It can't be easy with so many memories. I think he's very lonely.'

'Very angry and quite rude, too! Well, we'll just have to jolly him up at the quiz later.'

* * *

Despite some determined cheerfulness on Granny Jean's part, Ron was subdued that evening. Even Ben was quiet, other than insisting that the answer to every question had been on the tip of his tongue.

Holly thought that the bracing Hebridian air must have got to all of them, because their score reflected that none of them seemed very awake!

When the quiz had finished Ben and Holly went off to fetch tea and coffee for them all.

'What's wrong?' Ben asked as they stood silently waiting their turn at the hot-water dispenser.

'What do you mean? Nothing's wrong.'

'Could have fooled me. I thought we were okay now. That you'd decided that, after all, I could just about pass for being one of the human race. But now I'm getting the big freeze again.'

'You're exaggerating.' Holly avoided his eyes, trying to forget the shaky feeling she'd had earlier just looking into them.

'I'm a bit tired, that's all.'

He raked his fingers through his thick hair.

'Look, I'm not plotting to have my evil way with you, or propose to you — heaven forbid! I just want to be friends, that's all.'

Suddenly she felt angry.

Why was he always wrong-footing her like this? Asking her probing questions that she didn't want to answer — that she certainly had no intention of answering.

'You really are a pain in the neck, aren't you?' she said with a sudden burst of fury. 'I'm trying to be polite here, have a nice relaxed holiday with my granny. I didn't ask you to interfere! I didn't ask to be put on your table.

Why can't we just be polite to each other, without analysing the rest of it?'

' 'The rest of it'? Now, that's very interesting . . . what exactly do you mean by that?'

Holly sighed. Surely she didn't have to explain all over again?

Then she looked up and saw by his grin that, if he hadn't been joking at first, he most certainly was now.

'Sorry.' She poured herself some coffee. 'I guess I lost my sense of humour for a moment.'

'Blame Gramps,' Ben said. 'I always do.'

They joined their grandparents.

'Thanks, darling.' Granny Jean took her cup. 'I've just been looking on the list of what's taking place on board, and guess what? They're giving dance lessons!'

'I can dance,' Ron said suddenly. 'Used to dance with Sheila. We learned years ago, with Victor Sylvester's dance studios.'

'Did you, Ron?' Holly smiled. 'I've

always wanted to do ballroom dancing, you know.'

Granny Jean's eyes were shining.

'Why don't we all go? I can do a passable quickstep and the waltz, but I've always wanted to tango.'

Ben looked horrified.

'You're kidding, right?'

'No.' Granny Jean seemed quite unabashed. 'Not really. I watch it on the television. The dancers look so pretty, like fairies wafting around the floor.'

'That's what I'm afraid of,' Ben said.

Gramps gave an amused chuckle before rapidly resuming his habitual doleful expression.

'Sorry. Out of the question for me with this knee.'

'Oh, and I thought it was so much better!' Jean raised her eyebrows. 'I was watching you today, you managed those hill paths better than most men half your age.'

Ron flushed. 'Still have to be careful not to twist it though. It's like a knife going through me when that happens.'

'Hmm,' said Jean looking sceptical. 'Well, if you change your mind . . . I'm going anyway. I'll probably end up dancing with another woman, women are always braver than men over this kind of thing.'

'I'll think about it,' said Ron.

Just how stupid could you get? Ben scolded himself later. First of all, to question Holly like that, as though he cared that she was behaving a little bit frostily. And then to miss the opportunity to hold her in his arms under the pretext of learning to dance! What was the matter with him?

Furthermore, what was even worse was having said out loud that he didn't want to have his evil way with her or, worse — marry her. Not cool, Ben! What a crazy thing to say!

No wonder she looked at him as though she couldn't believe what she was seeing or hearing.

He'd been caught off guard when she stumbled, that was the trouble. Without even thinking about it, out had shot his hand. He'd gripped her elbow in just the way he would have gripped Granny Jean's elbow, or Gramps', in order to steady them.

But it wasn't so much the gripping as the letting go that had been difficult. It had taken a real effort to release her. Instead, he'd known a longing to hold on very tight, to pull her closer, to feel her warm supple body next to his, to taste her parted lips . . .

Enough, he told himself. Holly was a very attractive girl and he was, after all, human. But just because the desire was there you didn't have to act on any of it.

Pull yourself together and leave the poor girl alone, he reprimanded. You're nothing to her, and she's nothing to you. Pleasant travelling companions, ships that pass in the night, that's all. And that's good. Absolutely fine!

After saying he had work to do and excusing himself, Ben returned to his laptop to solve the problem of the dead body in the harbour-master's office.

* * *

Holly, meanwhile, didn't know what to think. She was thinking way too much, that was the trouble. From the start she had just known Ben was going to be . . . well, what? A nuisance? A distraction? A temptation, even? But, it hadn't turned out to be any of those things. It was just that he made her self-aware, somehow. Made her conscious of the fact that here she was, young, single, attractive — well, passably attractive, she amended, modestly — yet with no one in her life who made her heart beat faster.

But she didn't want anyone in her life to make her heart beat faster, did she? The last time that had happened it had been the office Lothario at the solicitors' firm where she worked, who'd been the cause of the raised tempo of her heartbeat. For a while, she'd even felt she might have the urge to settle down. It had been bliss for six months, until that particular obsession had linked up with the new litigation clerk.

Said litigation clerk had been a tall smouldering brunette, and after that, the whole thing had turned into an unmitigated disaster. Holly had been dumped quicker than you could blink and in order to save her pride, she had been the one to find another position.

That the new job had turned out, in addition to being more interesting, to be better paid was neither here nor there. It had been an inconvenience to her heart, and she wasn't about to let her heart be inconvenienced again, thank you very much, Ben Brown.

She was being too serious, though, she knew. Ben had practically said as much to her. But then, no sooner had she tried to keep it friendly but light, play it cool, in fact, than he had started accusing her of giving him the big freeze. Remembering this, Holly flushed with annoyance. Just because she hadn't monopolised his attention, hung on his every word and behaved in every way as though he was the most desirable creature on God's earth . . . So, now who was being serious? And after he'd actually spelled it out to her that 'serious' was the last thing that he was being! What was that all about?

All in all Holly was heartily relieved when she found herself on the opposite side of the circular dinner table to Ben that evening. She was polite, even friendly, but no more so than with Ron. After the show, which they'd taken to going to most evenings, she'd pleaded tiredness and gone straight to bed.

But once in bed, and listening to Granny's regular breathing, she stared into the darkness and wondered how on earth she could feel so confused about a person after scarcely knowing them a few days.

5

On waking next morning to discover they were docked at the isle of Mull, Granny Jean and Holly had taken one look at the prettily painted Georgian buildings encircling Tobermory harbour and decided to take the tender to the quayside. Holly had been relieved to discover from Granny Jean that Ben and Ron had opted for a trip to Torosay and the Mull railway.

Good, that should keep Ben Brown, with his disturbing light-eyed gaze, well out of her sight and her thoughts.

The trip to shore was slightly rocky, but the sky was a brilliant blue and the sun was shining as the tender landed at the slipway.

'Oh, look!' Granny Jean remarked. 'There's a boat trip around the islands, and it goes past the isle of Staffa!'

Her eyes gleamed triumphantly.

'So?' Holly came up behind her and started to read what was on the board propped up on the walkway.

'That's the island where Fingal's cave is. You know, the inspiration behind Mendelssohn's 'Hebrides' overture. I was telling you about it only the other day.'

'Oh, okay,' Holly said doubtfully. 'We'll go, if you like. If you haven't had enough of boats, that is!'

They went into the booking-office that was part of a souvenir shop at the head of the small pier.

'It's a marvellous day for the trip!' Granny Jean was full of enthusiasm. 'I feel as though, this way, I'll see the real Scotland, the wild Scotland.'

The trip was due to start in an hour, which was just enough time for them to walk round the harbour. They made several purchases, mainly of a hand-made nature, in the beautifully maintained tourist shops.

Holly kept a wary eye on the sky, but so far it remained a totally unblemished blue.

It wasn't that she minded going on the boat trip — she was quite looking forward to it, in a way. It was just that the boat looked rather small and the sea very cold.

But they'd been promised a glimpse of otters and seals, plus possible sightings of dolphins as well as many different seabirds. It all sounded perfectly exhilarating.

Why, then, did Holly feel unaccountably flat? For a moment she allowed herself to wonder what Ben was doing. He was probably chatting up Julie, the blonde, voluptuous member of the entertainment crew who, she had noted, had been in charge of the trip to Torosay castle. Yes, most likely.

Oh, well, who was she to disapprove? They both thought highly of themselves; they'd make a perfect match!

⋆ ⋆ ⋆

Although the sun shone obligingly, the sea trip turned out to be stunningly beautiful but windy. The colours of the scenic richness of the islands they circumnavigated were for ever changing, the landscapes morphing from rugged to smooth; from lilac and pink, to stern greys and ominous browns.

The clear, sparkling sea seemed at one moment a translucent turquoise, the next, deep purple as a shadow from the soaring cliffs above struck.

They passed by Staffa island, but didn't land.

The captain of the boat told them that Fingal's cave had a ceiling sixty six feet high, with smooth black columns of basalt rising from the sea like enormous organ pipes.

He also said that the island's original Gaelic name of An Uamn Ehinn, which means 'musical cave', was derived from the sounds of the sea echoing through the cave's depths.

'How wonderful,' Granny Jean cried. 'Can't you just imagine Mendelssohn, a dark forelock of hair over one eye, his frilled shirt rippling in the breeze, being put ashore here along with his piece of parchment and a quill pen?'

She sighed in ecstasy.

'I can just see him, sitting on an outcrop of rock with the sea crashing all around him, rushing to get all the music in his ears on to paper. It must have been wonderful!'

'I hope he didn't forget to bring a warm coat and some ink, too,' Holly said dryly. 'Quill pens didn't work like biros, you know!'

'You're so prosaic, Holly.' Granny Jean sniffed. 'You should just give yourself up to the romance of the situation, use your imagination. It's a shame Ben's not with us. I'm sure he'd understand what I mean.'

'Hmm,' Holly rejoined.

'What does he do anyway? For a living, I mean.'

'He's a sports journalist. Haven't you noticed the way he has to check up on the sports news all the time? Besides which, he's writing a thriller at the moment, not a romance.'

Granny's eyes widened.

'That's interesting. A thriller, eh? I've always wanted to write a thriller.'

Briefly, Holly wondered if there was anything Granny Jean hadn't always wanted to do!

'Yes, well, I think it's easier said than done. He's stuck at the moment. Has a dead body in the harbour-master's office and doesn't know how to get rid of it.'

'How did the man die?'

'There was a fight, apparently, and he knocked his head too hard on a filing cabinet.'

'I'll have to think about it, and try to come up with something. I'd love to see my words in print. Oh, look, is that a sea eagle?' Granny Jean went back to her binoculars and the constant look-out for wild life.

* * *

Ben had had a good morning.

He'd enjoyed the impressive Victorian

Torosay castle, which had been built in true Scottish baronial style, set as it was in acres of superb gardens with staggering views at every turn.

It had been fun to watch his grandfather drinking in the magnificence of the landscape and bracing air, and slowly starting to relax. He'd derived more than a little amusement, too, from watching Gramps slowly unbend under the insistent chaperonage of Julie, who was overseeing the excursion. On the twenty-minute train journey Julie had determinedly sat herself on the other side of Gramps, then had proceeded to chat about the local landmarks, for the most part addressing her remarks across him to Ben. Of course, his grandfather had blustered a bit, but he could see that he was quite enjoying the reflected glory of the attention.

Ben also knew that Gramps would be perfectly aware that the quarry Julie had in mind was actually his grandson, and realised that the fiendish delight

Gramps was taking in stringing her along was a very healthy sign that, at last, he was taking an interest — albeit a mischievous one — in what was going on around him.

If, occasionally, a picture of Holly with her bright smile and beguiling brown eyes popped into Ben's mind, he resolutely made sure it popped straight out again by applying his mind to the Scottish scenery instead. It was probably good for them to have a break from each other, he reasoned to himself. Very good indeed.

'Ben, are you listening?' It was Gramps. 'I was saying our timing's good. We'll go back to the Anastasia for a late lunch now, have a rest before afternoon tea, then there's the quiz. After that, we'll have just enough time to get ready for dinner and the show.'

'I see you have it all mapped out for me,' Ben said good-naturedly, 'but I think I'll have a look round Tobermory before I catch a tender back. The last one's not till four.'

'Suit yourself. I'll see you later.'

Ben watched from the shoreline as the old man, more upright, surely, than before, accepted a helping hand into the tender and then with a salute-like wave, settled himself down for the trip back to the Anastasia.

* * *

Ben heaved a sigh of relief and turned to inspect the waterfront with its row of quaint, sugared almond-coloured cottages. Glory be, could that be an angel coming out of a shop and towards him? And she was alone — unaccompanied by Granny Jean or any other passengers. Not only that, alleluia, she was smiling, too!

'You've missed the tender, I'm afraid,' he said. 'I've just seen Gramps onto it. He's frightened of missing out on his lunch.'

'No, I didn't miss it. Granny went back on the last one, muttering about dancing, but I'm not hungry. Anyway, I wanted to walk up the cliff path on the left there and take some photos.'

'Just what I had in mind,' Ben lied. 'I've been told the views are really good. Would you mind if I tagged along?'

It only took a moment's hesitation before she nodded and smiled.

They settled into an easy walking pace, which rapidly became a climbing pace as the hill became steeper.

Between puffing breaths, Holly told Ben about the boat trip and Granny's obsession with Mendelssohn, and Ben in turn furnished her with his morning's activities.

After that, they relapsed into silence, apart from the occasional grunt or groan from exertion.

The sun continued to shine brightly. Holly had taken her shower-proof jacket off and tied it round her waist; underneath it she was wearing a cream T-shirt — which fitted to perfection, Ben noted.

Eventually she stopped walking.

'I think we've missed the turning. I was told it was on the left. It must have been that scrubby little path I thought was going nowhere.'

Ben looked at the continuation of the road, which was bearing left but certainly couldn't be described as a cliff path.

'Well, how about we go along here anyway? We're up even higher, and probably still have a good view.'

They carried on walking, and pretty soon came to a building with the magic words Refreshments Available outside.

'Come on, I think a cup of tea's called for,' he said.

Holly was busy with her camera.

'You were right . . . Look, I can see the Anastasia from here!'

Ben stood and watched as she framed the photo, changed her mind about where she was standing, and eventually squatted down in order to take the shot. She certainly had a good figure, he decided before deciding to follow his own advice and keep it friendly, keep it light. No distractions.

He made his way up the steps to the teashop which turned out to be not so much a teashop, more an arts centre. There were more stairs inside the shop, the walls lined with splashy originals painted by a local artist. The colours fairly sizzled off the canvasses.

Ben heard Holly suck in her breath.

'These are something special.'

'You're interested in painting?'

'Well, I can't paint myself, but yes, I'm interested. Granny Jean's the one who's taken up painting. She'll be wild to have missed this.'

'I doubt she'd have made the climb. I'm still trying to catch my breath.'

'I bet she would have, if she'd known this was at the end of it.'

Halfway up the stairs, Holly paused.

'Just look at this. He's captured the strength of the rocks and the untamed water exactly. And look at that sky, it's fairly singing out to you.'

'You should write for the gallery. You have a nice line in prose.'

She blushed.

'Sorry. I got carried away.'

'No, it's nice to see your enthusiasm.'

'Just think, we could have missed all this, if we'd taken the right path,' Holly said some time later after she'd exhausted the shop's supply of canvasses, and had bought cards featuring reproductions of some of the pictures on display. They were now sitting in the top bay window of the shop, with a pot of tea on the table between them. 'Just look at this view.'

'I am.' Ben was studying her profile and thinking how beautiful it was. 'Believe me, I am.'

She felt herself colouring and refused to meet his eyes.

'What was the show like last night?' she asked, when the silence became unbearable.

'Oh, you didn't miss much. A few Barbara Streisand songs, an Elvis impersonation. 'Ah huh huh!' ' He curled his lip with a leer.

Holly spluttered into her tea.

‘That was the worst Elvis impersonation I’ve ever seen! I bet your grandad could do better.’

‘You know, I really love it when you laugh like that.’ The words were out before he could stop himself.

At once her smile faded.

He groaned and put his head in his hands.

‘Oh, no! That was merely a friendly observation. Anyone would have said it. You should laugh more often — it really is infectious.’

‘I do laugh, often. Believe me. Ha ha ha!’

‘Sorry, sorry. I don’t know what it is. As soon as I find myself in your vicinity I turn into a prize idiot and start talking gibberish!’

For a long moment their gazes locked, then a smile started in her eyes and made its way to her lips.

‘Oh, so you don’t like my smile, after all? That was just the idiot gibberish talking, in fact?’

Her hand was lying on the table top

very close to his own. On impulse he took it, and held it.

'Holly,' he said. 'In addition to be devastatingly attractive you can also be extremely annoying. Still, let me tell you that, compared to Gramps, you are a mere novice! I will not give up on you. You will, eventually, learn to put up with me. We have five more days left. Let's see if we can enjoy them, shall we?'

That's it! he thought. Deal with her as you would Gramps — as though she's a sweet but aggravating child! Just don't get the two of them mixed up and suggest she might like a lie-down in your cabin. She might get entirely the wrong idea!

He looked away from her, out at the view. The Anastasia did indeed look just like a model boat from here, and in the distance you could hardly see where the sky ended and the purple mountains began.

Then his eyes narrowed. The reason for that confusion in the distance, he realised, was that the purply grey haze was actually caused by rain clouds which were approaching rapidly.

'Come on,' he said to Holly. 'We'll have to run if we don't want to catch that lot!'

After an astonished glance at the darkening skies, she grabbed her bag.

'That came in fast. A minute ago there wasn't a cloud in sight!'

Together they moved at a smartish pace back along the road and down the hill. Halfway down the hill, the rain clouds burst. Ben zipped up his jacket and watched as Holly struggled to unfasten hers from around her waist. He stood behind her and helped her arms into the sleeves of her jacket, then, resisting the impulse to kiss the tip of her raindrop-covered nose, carefully did her up. They were out of breath and soaking wet by the time they reached the tender, which had been waiting for them at the very bottom of the quayside.

'You were lucky.' A lady in a plastic hood with rain on her spectacles was seated in the driest corner. 'You were spotted on the path, otherwise we would have gone without you. This is the last tender, you know!'

With a last disapproving look she turned her blue, plastic mac-covered back on them.

Giggling together like a couple of mischievous school children Ben and Holly squeezed into the only available space.

'You're very naughty,' he said in Holly's ear. 'Very naughty indeed — but I like you.'

6

Back on board, Holly and Ben prepared to go their separate ways. Between giggles she shivered, because the day that had started so brilliantly had now turned chilly as well as damp.

'Hot shower time, I think.'

'Good idea,' Ben agreed. He opened his mouth to say something further but, catching her eye, closed it again. He was learning, she suspected, not to come out with those awful one-liners. A couple of days ago he would have made some suggestive remark.

After her shower, she put on a long sweater and leggings and curled up on her bunk with a book. A little bit of peace and quiet was what she wanted, but somehow she couldn't seem to concentrate. Entirely uninvited, an image of Ben, with his wicked smile, kept coming between her and the printed page.

She remembered the sensation of his hand on her elbow, the way he'd oh, so gently zipped her into her jacket. The curiously intent way she'd caught him staring at her when he thought she wasn't looking, and the way that stare had made her feel. A hot feeling started in her stomach and flooded its way up to her face and down to her toes.

Impatiently, she snapped her book shut. Don't spoil a good thing, she told herself. He has backed off at your own request from trying to be romantic just because there's no one else around. He's content now to be just good friends. Which is what you wanted, after all.

Even so, the hot feeling didn't go away. She trembled as she remembered his breath in her ear.

'You are naughty — but I like you.'

Hardly romantic, but funny, and not at all contrived. Without being aware of it, Holly stored it up along with another handful of memories she would treasure from this trip.

There was the sound of footsteps outside in the gangway. Footsteps and a low laugh, followed by a fumbling at the door handle.

'Hello, darling.' Granny Jean entered the cabin in a smiling rush. 'I've had such a good time at the dance class . . . I've learned to tango! Would you believe it? The only thing is, I'm not quite sure what you tango to. I mean, everyone knows you cha-cha to Tea For Two and waltz to The Blue Danube. But tangos?'

She sat down on her bunk and eased her feet out of her shoes.

'Oh, that's better.' She massaged her toes. 'And how did you get on? I saw the rain come down, did you get very wet?'

Laughing, Holly assured her grandmother that no, she didn't get completely soaked, and that she'd met up with Ben who had turned out to be a bearable companion for the afternoon.

'You see? I told you he had another side. It's probably the writer in him. I was quite surprised, too, today. Ron's not so bad, once he gets chatting and forgets to be quite so sorry for himself.' She looked serious for a moment.

'Reading between the lines, I'd say he's suffering from guilt, that's why he's so crabby. He's reproaching himself, because he didn't tell Sheila how much he loved her. The poor bloke probably didn't even realise it himself until after she'd died.

'That's the trouble, when death's so sudden. You have no time to say what you should have said in all the years you had together. Then, after they've gone, you have all the time in the world to regret it.

'I was one of the lucky ones, although it didn't feel like that at the time. I told your grandfather over and over again how much I loved him, what a good marriage we'd had, what a worthwhile life we'd lived together . . . '

She drew a shaky breath.

'I went on telling him, even when I wasn't sure he could hear me any more. I had to.'

Her hand, as it rested on the blue blanket, trembled, and Holly covered it sympathetically with her own.

An apologetic laugh escaped Granny. Jean as she turned and gave her a quick hug.

'Afterwards, when it was all over, I often wondered why I said all that. Because it wasn't entirely true. He left me in the hell of a financial muddle . . . There were times when I was furious with him! But now, well, I look at Ron eating himself up with remorse, and I'm glad I did talk so much in those last days. It wasn't so much for me as for him, you see. It enabled him to go peacefully. I feel no guilt. I feel at peace, too, and free to enjoy myself.'

'And he'd want you to,' Holly assured her.

Her grandmother squared her shoulders.

'Right, come on. I have to get my glad rags on and so do you, and then we'll go out and enjoy ourselves tonight — won't we?'

* * *

On the whole, the day had gone well, Ben thought.

Okay, they had missed the quiz. But, surprisingly, Gramps hadn't seemed to mind too much about that.

Ben had found out that, instead of going to the quiz, Gramps had looked in on the progress of the ballroom dance classes, and had immediately been snaffled by Julie as one daring to be bold and have a go at something new.

Amazingly, Gramps had obliged in partnering her, and had soon been floating around the room, all traces of a twisted knee temporarily forgotten.

On his return to the ship and upon finding an empty cabin, Ben had taken advantage of the time to apply himself to his laptop.

Unfortunately, though, he still hadn't been able to resolve the problem of the body in the harbour-master's office.

He did, however, manage a half-decent scene involving the hero and the 'maybe' heroine becoming caught in a storm, which resulted in their having to remove their clothing and huddle together for warmth!

The end of the dance lesson and Gramps's subsequent return put a stop to any more detailed description.

Perhaps just as well! Ben decided. The heroine kept showing a tendency to appear like Holly.

All in all, he was quite ready for a hearty evening meal and whatever else the night might have to offer. Then he found it was indeed his lucky day, for, on entering the dining-room, at their table Holly was sitting next to the only vacant seat.

'Well, well, well. Can anyone sit here?'

'Of course not, but you can. Sit yourself down.' Granny Jean spoke from the other side of Holly. 'I've been giving your dilemma some thought.'

'Ah,' Ben responded without having the faintest idea what she was speaking about.

'The body, and how to dispose of it . . . You know, in your book. It's definitely dead, is it?'

'As a door nail.' Ben poured himself some wine.

'Well, why don't you drag him — is it a him? — right, drag him out in the dead of night, leaving a trail of blood, or not, as you like. Then dump it — him — over the side of the dock! A boat could come in, and have the effect of crushing the body completely and unrecognisably, if you like.'

Granny Jean's eyes glistened.

'What do you think?'

'And I thought you were a nice little old lady!'

She patted her hair modestly.

'I watch a lot of crime dramas.'

'Gramps likes watching police dramas,' he said. 'Don't you, Gramps?'

'Sometimes.' Ron was busy studying the menu.

'He usually works out who's done it pretty fast, as well.'

'Really?' Granny Jean said. 'I was

telling Holly I've always fancied writing a thriller. Not sure where to start, though, that's the trouble.'

'You have to start at the end and work backwards,' Holly put in. 'At least that's what I've heard.'

'Ah.' Ben clapped his hand to his head in mock surprise. 'That's where I've been going wrong!'

He winked at Granny Jean, helped himself to a bread roll and prepared to enjoy his meal.

* * *

The evening passed pleasantly enough. After dinner and the show, all the guests at their table went together to The Imperial Bar, only to discover Julie, in full throttle, belting out a Sixties number.

Ben spotted a table in a less well-lit area at the back, and guided them to it. By the time they'd settled themselves down and ordered drinks, the song had come to an end and Julie's debonair male counterpart was crooning something a little quieter and slower into the microphone.

Ben was just about to ask Holly whether she'd risk a dance with him when Julie arrived at their table.

'How are you?' She was addressing Gramps yet somehow Ben knew the question was directed at himself.

'I'm very well, thank you,' Ron replied. 'It takes more than a tango lesson to wear me out.'

'I was hoping you'd dance with me,' Julie went on, batting her heavily mascaraed lashes. 'But maybe you're about to dance with your . . . '

She glanced at Granny Jean, who promptly gave a snort of laughter.

'We're not married. Not yet, anyway,' Jean added saucily, seeing Ron's expression which could only be described as aghast.

Julie rolled her eyes and threw her head back.

'Ha, ha, ha! Touched a raw nerve, did I? Well, now's your chance, um, Jean, isn't it? You can get Ron on the dance floor. And, as you seem to be taken, Ron, perhaps your grandson will oblige me?' she continued relentlessly, turning to Ben.

Ben sent up a silent prayer for someone, anyone, please, to grab the girl's attention.

'He can't dance,' said Gramps. 'Two left feet. But I'll dance with you, if my knee will co-operate.'

Julie was too well trained to show anything other than mild displeasure.

'I'd be delighted,' she said through a tightly clenched smile.

Of course, Ben realised, the only reason Gramps had risen to the challenge was because he didn't know what to say to Granny Jean, after being mistaken for her husband. But watching the old man rise to his feet and escort Julie to the dance floor, out of gratitude he made the resolution never to moan about his grandfather again!

Granny Jean was still chuckling.

'That was priceless. Did you see the

look of horror on his face?'

'You're a wicked old woman.'

Holly wasn't laughing quite so much, Ben noticed. He wondered if it was too much to hope that the reason was because she didn't care too much for the idea of him dancing cheek-to-cheek with Julie.

Oh, how he hoped so.

7

It was two days later and day number seven of the cruise. Only three more days to go. Holly could hardly believe the time was passing so quickly.

The day before, that both Holly and her grandmother had looked forward to so much, had proved to be a wash out. The weather, considering it was June, was appalling. Despite the wall-to-wall rain, they had optimistically boarded the courtesy coach, which was to take them to the centre of Dublin. But when they got there the first thing they had been forced to do was to buy umbrellas.

Then, in an effort to stay dry yet still soak up a little of Dublin's history, they'd boarded a city tour bus. The bus windows had poured with water, and rain from passengers' clothes had soaked into the velour upholstery. Still Granny Jean had refused to be defeated. Holly had watched with admiration as she'd sat, perched on the edge of her seat, rain dripping off the end of her nose, her glasses steamed up from the atmosphere, but still listening intently to the commentary and ready with a bright smile every time a joke was made.

'Well, how very interesting,' she had said to Holly when finally there was a lull in the soft Irish narration, a chink was glimpsed in the heavy clouds and it had looked as though the rain might ease. 'I never knew all that about Molly Malone, although I did always wonder if the selling of cockles and mussels was her only trade! I mean, did you notice how low her neckline was on the statue?' She chuckled.

'Look, the clouds are breaking up, I think we should get off, now that the weather looks brighter, and maybe visit the botanical gardens.'

But it was not to be. No sooner had Granny finished speaking, than another burst of rain had come down, so they'd stayed on the bus until they had completed the circuit. Peering through the streaming windows, it was with difficulty that they'd made out the fine Georgian houses in Merrion Square, or even the River Liffey, where they had agreed to give their planned river trip a miss.

Oh, well, as Granny Jean had pointed out, at least they hadn't paid for it in advance. After braving a drizzly Grafton Street, dodging between raindrops into some of the beautiful shops, because Granny Jean's favourite Irish authors had inspired her not to miss the largest city square in Europe, they had looked at one another in their bedraggled state and had agreed to call it a day.

Holly, suddenly aware that she'd been subconsciously searching for a glimpse of Ben all the time they'd been in Dublin, had been in a subdued mood as they'd made their way back to join the others at the pick-up point.

The rest of the day had been equally disappointing. Later in the afternoon they'd gone to attend the quiz, only to find that, in the hope that the weather would improve, Gramps and Ben had gone into Dublin rather later than they had themselves, and weren't yet back.

Furious with herself for being disappointed, Holly had insisted that they should still participate in the quiz, and they'd teamed up with another table, only to be mortified when their results were lamentably poor.

'Oh, dear,' Granny Jean had wailed. 'We'd better make a pact not to mention the word quiz. Ron would crow with delight if he knew how badly we did without him!'

But, when they had finally met up at the dinner-table, Ron had been surprisingly chipper. It had transpired that, after a visit to a museum and to The National Art Gallery, he and Ben had spent a considerable amount of time in Dublin's famous breweries and pubs!

Apparently, from time to time Ben had put his nose out of the door in order to find out if the weather had improved. The unrelenting rain, however, he had said, had made the only sensible option staying put, glass in hand, for most of the day.

Consequently, both men that evening had looked slightly bloodshot around the eyes, and had been heavily occupied in swallowing yawns.

'I hope we're not keeping you up,' Holly had remarked tartly on one occasion, when Ben had failed to smother a really gigantic yawn.

'Look, you can't visit Ireland without sampling their most famous brew,' Ben had pointed out. 'Anyway, the thought of accompanying Gramps on an all day excursion in the rain, with no alcoholic relief, was just too much to be contemplated. Can you imagine the misery he'd put me through?'

The yawning had soon proved to be catching and, after the show which Ben and Gramps, probably due to an excess of alcohol, had chosen to avoid, Holly and her grandmother, who had admitted to being rather tired, had decided to have an early night.

* * *

Now, the dawning of day seven was proving to be far more encouraging, with sizzling sunshine and a cloudless sky. At this moment Holly was making the most of it, sitting on a low stone wall in the beautiful abbey gardens of Tresco. Her shoulders were feeling pleasantly warm, and her feet delightfully free in open-toed sandals.

At last, now they'd arrived at the Scilly Isles, it felt like June.

'This is more like it.' Ben was sitting next to her, his face turned to the sun, his bare legs stretched out next to hers. Hers, she noticed, were distinctly pale compared to his.

'How did your legs get so brown?' she asked, before she'd even considered that someone not meant to be taking an interest in another person would hardly make such a query.

'Oh, I go to the tanning salon once a week,' he answered casually.

'You don't!'

'No, you're right — I don't! I was in New Zealand in February, and got lucky with the weather. Since then they've sort of stayed brown. I've been careful not to wash them, of course.'

'What were you doing in New Zealand?'

Ben looked at her from under lazy lids.

'Having a great time mainly. Did a bit of trekking, a bit of work in the tourist trade. Wrote a few pieces for various sports magazines. You know — scuba-diving, bungy-jumping, white water-rafting, that sort of thing.'

Holly stared at him in amazement. There was a lot more to Ben Brown than she'd thought. In February on the other side of the world, living the independent life of a free spirit, and now in June watching out for his grandfather on a cruise which, although by no means regimented, must be a complete contrast to his last adventurous enterprise.

And to think she'd once thought of

him as shallow. Thinking of her own safe life, Holly blushed.

'You never said.'

'You never asked. Anyway, there's no-one so boring as a person who goes on and on about all the places they've been to. Specially someone you meet on holiday. Before you know it, it turns into a 'have you been to?' contest. You know what I mean.'

He put on a high, falsetto upper-class accent.

''Oh, haven't you been to The Seychelles? You really must. It was so, so, wonderful, we really liked it. Had a marvellous time. Absolutely fabulous!' You must have met people like that, surely?'

'I suppose so.' Holly laughed. 'But I'd still like to hear about it. I've always wanted to go to New Zealand.'

'Well, in that case, how long have you got? No, I'll tell you another day and bore you with my maps and photos, too. But no, I don't have them with me. That really would be crass, wouldn't it

— to come on holiday bringing the last holiday's photos with me? Anyway . . . ' He cast a quick glance down at his wrist watch.

'We'd better start back down these steps. Poor Granny Jean will be tearing her hair out trying to amuse Gramps, and he'll be glowering into his garden map wondering what's taking us so long.'

He leaned over and reached for Holly's hand. His fingers were warm and brown. He pulled her to her feet, then, with an expression of disbelief in his eyes, held on to her hand for longer.

Lacking the will to pull away, Holly found herself gazing into his light hypnotic eyes. In a moment, she thought, I'll blink, and when I open my eyes the moment will be lost, the magic gone, and the sun will have disappeared.

Ben didn't blink, either.

'You're amazing,' he said softly, drinking her in with his eyes. With the index finger of his other hand he gently traced the contour of her face.

Holly couldn't have moved, even had she wanted to. The world around her seemed suffused in a rosy glow. She was dimly aware of the sun on her back, the flowers in their striking blues, pinks and oranges all around them, the sky up above, the sea far below. No sound of traffic or voices or aeroplanes, only the small sounds of insects buzzing and a faint breeze stirring the cotton shrubs at the side of the path.

Eventually she did blink, and when she opened her eyes it seemed impossible to look away from his lips, firm, half open in a smile, coming slowly towards hers.

She didn't want this kiss to happen. But she didn't want it to stop. Although it was so soft, so gentle, so undemanding, she wanted it to go on and on exactly like that — on and on, without stopping.

Reluctantly, Ben pulled away.

Don't say anything, she thought. Not a word; nothing to spoil it all. Not an apology — that would be too awful. Not 'I didn't mean that to happen'. And above all, please don't make a silly joke.

He did none of those things, just stared at her, as though perhaps he'd never really seen her before

She broke the stare, took a step backwards and picked up her bag. Then she turned and together, not touching one another, they made their way back down the steep path in silence.

What exactly did you do that for? Ben asked himself, taking care not to look her straight in the eyes as they negotiated the steep steps and winding paths back to the garden café in a trance-like silence. Have you taken leave of your senses? Why upset a perfectly good friendship in that way?

But he'd wanted so much to kiss her, and as for Holly, well, she really was just asking to be kissed, looking so lovely, so natural and so completely irresistible. Didn't she realise that, sitting there on the pale terracotta wall, just glorying in the sun with her head thrown back, she looked sweet, and utterly desirable?

No man could have resisted her. It wasn't as though there had been any planning involved. It had just happened. One moment he'd been seeking to break the mood, resist the temptation he knew was there, by pulling her to her feet. The next? Well, the next moment he'd wanted time to stand still. He had wanted that first taste of her soft, salt-flavoured lips to last for ever.

* * *

It was a relief to reach the garden's café and comparative normality. They found both grandparents sitting at a table with a couple of elderly ladies from the Anastasia. As usual, Granny Jean was in full flow, discussing the beauties of the island and the history of the abbey gardens which, she informed anyone in earshot, were laid out on the site of a tenth-century Benedictine monastery.

One look at his grandfather's face told Ben that his energy was at a low ebb. With a twinge of conscience, he snapped himself back into the present wondering whether he should feel guilty for more or less forcing Gramps to come on this trip and whether it was doing him any good at all.

'You okay, Gramps?'

'Hmm,' came the reply.

'Tired, I expect. I know I am!'

'Well, my ears could do with a rest.' Gramps looked meaningfully in the direction of Granny Jean.

Luckily, his remark seemed to go unheard. Ben stole a sidelong glance at Holly's delectable profile. She had developed a few freckles over her nose, he noticed. He wondered if she felt as bowled over as he did, or whether she had just thought of the kiss as being casual and friendly. Which it was, he reassured himself — exactly that, just casual and friendly. No need to work himself up in to such a lather about it. Absolutely not.

As though feeling his gaze on her, Holly turned and, for the first time since the kiss, looked straight into his eyes. It was as much as Ben could do not to gasp out loud. Granny Jean was still rattling on in the background, chairs were being pulled out, Gramps was struggling to find his stick. Ben was aware of all those things. But, for some reason, his brain was saying over and over, 'My brown-eyed girl, my brown-eyed girl.'

Never taking his eyes from Holly's face, he groped for his grandfather's walking-stick.

'Here's your stick, Gramps,' his mouth said while his brain was still saying 'My brown-eyed girl' over and over.

Holly looked away first.

'Yes,' she said in answer to some question Ben had been oblivious to. 'We'd better head for the ferry.'

A straggle of passengers made their way on board the ferry, which was waiting to take them back to St Mary's.

'No dancing tonight,' Granny Jean announced as Ben helped her, then Gramps, on board. 'All that walking has made my legs ache. Worth it, though. Shame we couldn't make it right to the top, the view must have been beautiful. Still, some of the lower gardens were wonderful, so colourful. Wouldn't you agree, Ron?'

He gave a grunt.

'I don't see as well as I used to.'

'Is that so?' Granny Jean asked. 'Well, you should get something done about it.'

'That's all very well for you to say.' He pulled himself up straighter at the ferry rail. 'You don't have to go through the procedure.'

'Well, actually Ron, no I don't. Because I already have, and it was the best thing I've ever done. My sight was appalling; it was a blight on my life. But I've had an operation, only a little while ago, and now I appreciate all the wonderful things around me, clearly instead of through a blur. I'm now able to appreciate my wonderful life.'

Get out of that, Gramps, Ben thought.

'Well, obviously, you've been lucky enough to enjoy good health apart from your eyesight,' Ron retorted, visibly bristling. 'I'm afraid we're not all so fortunate. There's not one part of me that's functioning correctly.'

Granny Jean gave a naughty smile.

'Except for your mouth. That appears to be in full working order.'

There was a deathly hush, during which time Ben was aware of Holly holding her breath.

He watched Gramp's profile. It was touch and go.

Suddenly the corner of the old man's mouth twitched and he gave a short bark of laughter.

'Good.' Granny Jean nodded. 'You're not entirely decrepit then — at least you've still got your sense of humour.'

8

For some reason Holly wasn't entirely sure of, Ben seemed to be avoiding eye contact. Well, perhaps she wasn't being entirely honest with herself there, because she herself was feeling unaccountably shy of meeting his glance. But every time she did risk a sly peep she received the impression that he knew she was looking at him and was choosing to ignore it. And the only reason she could come up for him ignoring her was that he regretted that kiss.

Well, she didn't regret it, she thought defiantly. She'd enjoyed every moment of it. Because — oh, might as well admit it — it was the best kiss she'd ever had in her life!

Not the most passionate, or even the most romantic. There had been no moonlight of course, no music in the background. She hadn't wafted in on a cloud of perfume, or been dressed to kill. Ben hadn't just had a shave, he'd been dressed even more casually than herself, in a creased shirt and faded shorts, while as for his sandals, well, they'd looked as though they were about to disintegrate.

There had been no waves crashing on a beach either. Only the buzz of a bee and the pounding of her own heart in her ears. He hadn't pulled her closer so that their hearts beat as one, or murmured words of love and undying devotion.

No, none of those things. It had just been a touch, a whisper of a kiss. Warm lips on lips, and a sweetness that had filled her soul. Romance with a capital R.

Now, Holly looked at her reflection in the mirror of the ladies' room and wondered where they would go from here.

The evening's suggested dress code had been casual, but her scoop-necked top showed off the fresh tan on her throat and shoulders, her eyes held a certain sparkle and she knew she was looking her best.

And what had it all been for? she asked herself despondently. Ben had been preoccupied in talking to Granny Jean and Gramps, to the ex-policeman's wife, the Rumanian waiter, the person on the next table . . . anyone, in fact, other than Holly!

Finally, out of desperation, she'd escaped from the table to the ladies' room in an effort to restore her calm and talk some sense into herself.

She hadn't even liked Ben up until now, for heaven's sake. She'd thought him too opinionated, too openly mocking, too attractive and too aware of the fact. Too everything, really.

She'd been wrong. He was attractive, but he was also nice. Not easy to be nice when you've come on a holiday with a grandparent as ungrateful as Ron, she had to admit, often was. But Ben had been unfailingly light-hearted about it all, and it was obvious, despite the sparring between them, that the relationship with his grandfather was a good one.

Just why had she choked him off so often and so rudely? He was only trying to be friendly. Okay, so he might have been looking for a little flirtatious interlude, to brighten up ten days spent on board a cruise ship full of older people.

Well, what right had she to be hoity toity about that? Why couldn't she have just gone along with it? A few kisses never hurt anyone. In fact, as she'd now discovered, they could even do you a power of good!

So, loosen up, Holly, she scolded herself. Fix a bright smile on your lips and see if you can enjoy the last couple of days you have left with Ben.

Once a new coat of lipstick had been applied with an unsteady hand, Holly prepared to go back to the dinner table.

* * *

Ben jerked suddenly awake. After tossing and turning for what felt like hours, he'd finally drifted into a troubled sleep. In his dream he'd felt that there was something he was looking for, and that it was imperative he found whatever it was very soon, or it would be lost for ever.

Now he turned over, then struggled to sit up. Because the humped shape in the opposite bunk was missing. There was no light showing under the bathroom door, either.

Wide awake now, with a heart that was beating uncomfortably fast, Ben struggled against the unsteadiness of the ship to don jeans and a sweater. He pushed his feet into his sandals.

They had both decided on an early night, Gramps because he was tired, Ben because he'd wanted to avoid Holly.

Holly was just too attractive, with lips that were too kissable for Ben to be comfortable with until he'd got his head round the idea that never seeing her again in two days' time was a frightening, lonely prospect.

The thing was, it hadn't been frightening. Not until the kiss. Only a moment before that kiss he'd been toying with the idea of maybe meeting up with her in Colchester, where they both worked, of lending her a CD of his New Zealand photos, having a laugh over this holiday.

But now, since the kiss, Ben was having second thoughts. A romantic dalliance on board was one thing; a matey friendship afterwards also acceptable; but a full-blown love affair where feelings were involved?

Still, back to the current problem. Of course, Gramps had only stepped outside for a breath of fresh air. Of course he had. Unlike Ben, Gramps had fallen asleep immediately, proceeding to snore for England. He'd probably woken up with cramp in his leg, and decided, in a rare moment of unselfishness, that he didn't want to disturb his grandson, so had gone outside for some exercise.

Yes, that would be it. Bound to be.

Shaking slightly, Ben put his wallet and his swipe door card in his pocket and let himself out of the cabin. There was no sign of Gramps in the corridor. Best check the deck they were on first, then. Gingerly, Ben pushed open the heavy door leading to the outside deck. What felt like a force nine gale blasted round his ears, making his eyes smart. Surely Gramps wouldn't be out here, braving the elements in these sorts of conditions? He'd have to be off his head!

Trying to fight down images of his tall but too-thin grandfather toppling overboard, Ben ducked back inside again. No, Gramps would likely be sitting in the radio room, where a screen showing the ship's progress held a constant fascination for him. Wishing that the English Channel wasn't proving to be quite so choppy tonight, Ben swayed his way towards the middle of the ship.

His eyes swept the small radio lounge.

At first he didn't see him, though he was quite surprised to see a handful of fellow insomniacs had taken refuge there. In one corner were two old ladies, bundled up in shawls, who appeared to be semi-conscious, in another a rather large man sat doing a crossword puzzle.

Then Ben heaved a sigh of relief as he spotted his grandfather slumped in a chair, doing what he did best — staring at the screen which was plotting the ship's progress.

He felt faint with relief. Thank God.

'Hi, Gramps. You gave me quite a scare,' he said quietly, sliding himself into a seat next to him.

Gramps looked at him with tired eyes.

'Can't think why. I never asked you to be my nursemaid on this trip.'

Ben gave a grin.

'See you're still on form.'

After a long moment Gramps gave a grunt and mutter, which sounded almost like an apology.

His grandson couldn't help teasing

him. His eyebrows raised a notch.

'Did I hear you correctly? You didn't say 'sorry', did you?'

Gramps gave a wintry smile.

'No need for sarcasm.'

'No, I know. But seriously, Gramps, you had me worried for a minute. I wondered what on earth had happened to you.'

For a moment their eyes met, and Gramps cleared his throat.

'Suppose you think I'm a selfish old so and so.'

'Sometimes we're all selfish. I reckon you're entitled.'

'No. I'm not.' He looked away, then carried on in a milder tone. 'I know I'm an awkward cuss. Never been known for my tact, or my manners . . . Can't seem to help it, somehow. Got worse since your grandmother died.'

'Gramps, go easy on yourself. It was a shock . . . She wasn't even ill. None of us expected it.'

'I should have known. She only went out to get the washing in. I went to find out why she was taking so long, and that was it. Found her unconscious on the grass, just like that. I'll never forget it, never! Died in the ambulance with me holding her hand. Huh! Fat lot of good I was.'

'Gramps, don't do this,' Ben said.

The old man sighed.

'I know. I'm being unfair to everyone. Even your mother. Specially your mother.' He took a sideways glance at Ben. 'You're like her, you know. You've got time for people, same as your mother, same as Sheila. I always thought I was the strong one in our marriage. Turns out I'm the weak one. All I can see are all those long days stretching out before me. Sometimes I'm not sure I can face them.'

Feeling there was nothing he could say that would make matters any better, Ben stretched out a hand to cover the long, worn fingers resting on the arm of his chair.

'Women seem to cope better on their own,' Gramps went on. 'Your friend

Holly's grandmother, for example. She's always so cheerful. She understands, though, I think. She told me I should take one day at a time; make sure I have something planned to look forward to. A day out, a visit, or a lunch.

'She said that, anyway, as you get older life gets like a helter-skelter. It goes faster and faster, and you know there's bound to be a bump at the bottom, but hey, what's the use in thinking about that?'

'Sounds like Granny Jean.' Ben found himself suddenly yawning widely, now that the fear of finding Gramps lying in a crumpled heap somewhere had retreated.

His grandfather looked at him, and with a sudden unexpected gesture leaned forward and ruffled his hair.

'We'd best get back and get some rest,' he said gruffly. 'I appreciate your coming on this trip with me, you know. Should have said it before, I know that.'

Momentarily Ben's mouth gaped with astonishment. Was that really a thank you? Then he noticed that Gramps's eyes looked suspiciously bright.

He swallowed.

'Come on, Gramps, you're getting overtired.'

His voice was gruff to hide the fact that there was a sudden prickling in his throat which threatened to bring tears to his own eyes.

* * *

The next day found the Anastasia at anchor near Guernsey's capital of St Peter Port. Holly and Granny Jean were going on an island trip, which included a cream tea.

Over the buffet breakfast, where Granny Jean had bumped into Ben at the bacon counter, she had gleaned that he and his grandfather were going to visit the German Military Underground Hospital at Vassalerie, and the museum in Forest.

'Typical man stuff,' she told Holly dismissively. 'I'd much rather be looking at beautiful beaches and lovely countryside than examining underground tunnels hewn out of solid rock.'

She gave a shiver.

'I don't understand why people want to dwell on such things. We should look forwards, not backwards.'

'Well, each to their own.' Holly was feeling unsettled and rather argumentative. 'We have to learn from our history and our past mistakes. We don't have to dwell, exactly, but it could be quite interesting.'

'You could have gone with Ben if you'd wanted to, darling,' Granny Jean said. 'You know I can always find someone to pal up with.'

Holly flushed.

'No. You're right, it's much too beautiful a day to be cooped up inside museums and the like. Anyway, I don't particularly want to go anywhere with Ben and, more to the point he doesn't want to go anywhere with me.'

Granny Jean gave her an appraising glance.

'Do you feel okay? You seem a bit

down in the mouth.'

'Oh, I'm all right. I just don't know what I've done to upset Ben. You saw what he was like last night at dinner.' She bit her lip and sniffed. 'He hardly said a word to me all evening.'

'Perhaps he was tired,' Granny suggested comfortingly. 'Ron can be a very wearing companion, you know.'

'Yes, but he didn't even look at me. Not that I mind that, of course. It's not as though I care what he does!'

'Of course not,' Granny Jean agreed hastily.

'Although he seemed very keen to be friendly at the beginning of the trip, you know.'

'Well, I suppose that's it.' Holly sighed. 'It's only a holiday friendship, after all. Ships that pass in the night, and all that sort of rubbish. I suppose he's scared that, as we both work in Colchester, I'll ask him for his mobile number or something.'

She tried to shut out the recollection that Ben had actually mentioned showing her his photos of New Zealand at some time, because he didn't have them with him here on the cruise. Instead, Holly smiled determinedly.

'Anyway, I'm not going to waste time on Ben Brown when we have a lovely day ahead of us. I'm going to work on topping up my tan!'

* * *

That evening, Holly wished she hadn't worked quite so hard on the plan to tan. She had neglected to allow for the sea breeze factor, and when she dressed for dinner she found that her shoulders were scorching and her face felt like a furnace.

'I did suggest that you should wear a hat,' Granny Jean said smugly as Holly tried to tone down the fiery red of her nose and cheeks.

'All right, goody two shoes,' Holly replied.

She looked in admiration at her grandmother's lightly tanned complexion, which set off her sparkling eyes and silver hair to perfection.

'You look really great, Granny. You'll have all the old men after you!'

'I'd rather have a young one,' Granny answered, winking shamelessly.

However, by the time Holly had brushed her hair until it gleamed and wriggled herself into a long, cream silky dress, she had to admit her own reflection was looking more impressive.

Not only did she feel glowing on the inside, she glowed on the outside.

Well, even if Ben never wanted to see her again, at least she would know she'd looked pretty knock-out gorgeous on more than one occasion at the dinner table.

But when they reached the dining-room both Ben and his grandfather were conspicuous by their absence.

'I hope Ron's not acting up,' Granny Jean said. 'I wouldn't put it past him to feign a headache to get out of wearing his monkey suit, as he calls it.'

'I'm sure he wouldn't do that.' Holly spoke through gritted teeth. 'They've probably decided they'd rather eat at the buffet tonight. I don't blame them, really. It's a bit of a fag getting dressed up.'

'You put in so much effort, too, and you look good enough to eat. Never mind — the night is young. I think there's a night off for the dancers, and Julie will be singing the Barbra Streisand songs at the show.'

'Well, I wouldn't want to miss that,' Holly said with a fixed smile.

'If Ben and Ron aren't there we can go on to the Imperial Bar tonight afterwards, can't we?'

'Of course.'

* * *

What's the matter with me? she thought later as she followed her grandmother to see the evening show.

'Holly! Over here.'

Holly looked round, and her heart jumped into her throat. Gramps was beckoning to her and next to him, in an open-necked casual shirt, with a big smile all over his face, sat a sunburnt Ben.

'Fell asleep out on deck,' he admitted. 'Gramps didn't wake me up because we had a disturbed night last night. Sorry about dinner. We didn't have time to get changed — we only just made it to the buffet, and ate what was left before it shut.'

'Oh,' was all Holly could think to say.

'See? I told you there would be a reasonable explanation.'

Feeling ridiculously happy, for no logical reason that she could think of, Holly sat down next to Ben, accepted a gin and tonic and listened in a trance as Granny Jean and Ron started their normal sparring over who had had the best day.

Ben doesn't hate me, she thought. In fact, the way he looked at me just now, I'd even say he rather likes me! Thank heavens, he would never know how much she was blushing. The sunburn disguised that fact admirably.

He leaned forward, as though to say something to her, but just at that moment the lights went down. Wrapped in a skin-tight, sequinned sheath dress, Julie appeared on stage.

The girl could certainly hold her audience. She had a strong voice and a compelling presence. Even Holly was impressed. The audience, after a rapturous applause led by Gramps, demanded an encore. Very graciously, Julie obliged, this time singing a soulful ballad and staring rather markedly in Gramps direction.

But Holly wasn't too sure it was only Gramps she was focusing on. After all, Ben was sitting next to him.

After the show, Gramps was full of praise for Julie's performance.

'Very talented girl,' he kept saying. 'Very talented indeed. Did you see the way she was staring over at us? I think she might fancy me!'

Granny Jean gave a snort of laughter.

'She's too young for you,' Ben said with a grin.

'Says who?'

'Your doctor, I should think.' Ben handed him his stick. 'You nearly went without this, didn't you?'

Holly followed Granny Jean and Gramps out of the theatre, only realising when they were halfway along the gangway leading towards the Imperial Bar that she'd left her evening bag behind. Drat, she thought, she'd have to go back and get it.

Quickly, she explained to Granny Jean that she would catch her up in the bar. Then she hurried back to the theatre. Ben had gone to the men's room, she guessed, because he was nowhere in sight.

The theatre was now deserted, with only very subdued side lights to light her way. Trying to remember the exact seat she'd occupied, she walked down the aisle.

Ah, she could see her bag sparkling on the floor. She bent down to retrieve it.

Her face felt hot. She decided she

must take a breath of air on deck, just to cool her burning face a little. Then she could hot-foot it back to the bar, perhaps to take a deliciously, long, slow dance with the most attractive man on this ship.

The same man who, she had discovered, was the best kisser of all time — Ben Brown.

She pushed open the heavy deck door. Ah, that was better. Never mind that her hair was being blown into a wild bush, her floaty scarf nearly being snatched away by the breeze. The cool air was more than welcome on the heat of her cheeks.

Gracious, there was a courting couple standing, heads close together, their arms entwined in the shadow of a lifeboat.

How sweet. How romantic.

Then Holly froze. There was a low laugh, and the moonlight caught on the sequins of a dress she recognised instantly.

Holly's eyes widened. The dark-haired man was one Holly recognised. A pair of pale supple arms reached up behind his head, pulling him down.

Not wanting to see any more — Holly fled. The man with Julie, the hostess with the mostest, had been Ben.

9

What to do? What to do? Glassy-eyed, reeling as though she'd been shot, Holly made her way unsteadily to the Imperial Bar.

Thank goodness for the sunburn. She was sure that, without it, everyone would have guessed at the tumult in her mind and the pain in her heart.

Well, it was her own fault, she told herself severely. Hadn't she known from the very outset that Ben Brown would be trouble? It was no good snivelling now; no good swallowing and wishing she could just have a good cry. Whether or not that would come before or after she'd pushed him overboard she was not yet sure!

Meanwhile, how to get through the rest of the evening? Holly swallowed again. She could do this.

At least it wasn't as bad as having a

whole office witness your humiliation. This was at least relatively private.

Squaring her shoulders, and with a fixed smile on her lips, Holly kept moving along the corridor.

Luckily, when she reached the bar she found Granny Jean deep in conversation with Ron. At any other time Holly would have questioned this, but now she was only grateful for it.

Eventually her grandmother turned to her with a smile.

'All right, Holly? Did you find it?'

Holly gaped at her grandmother.

'What? Oh, my bag . . . Yes, yes, thanks, it was under my seat.'

Granny Jean was looking at her oddly.

'Are you okay, darling? Would you like another gin and tonic? Not had too much sun, have you?'

Bless Granny Jean for providing the perfect get out. Holly blinked rapidly and met her grandmother's expression of enquiry with one of innocence.

'Actually, you're right, I'm not feeling

so good. I feel a bit queasy.' She pulled a wry face. 'As you say, too much sun so no, I don't think another gin and tonic would be a good idea. I'm going to have to go back to the cabin and lie down.'

'Oh, what a disappointment.' Granny was immediately all concern. 'I knew you should have worn a hat! I'll come back with you.'

'No!' Holly almost shouted. 'I mean, no, thanks.'

She dropped her voice and gave a tremulous smile. 'I've developed a headache, too. You were right about the hat, I admit it. Now, don't worry, I'll be fine. I'll sleep it off.'

'Well, I won't be long behind you.' Granny Jean lowered her voice. 'I'll just stay long enough to be sociable.'

'Don't let me spoil your evening . . . I just need a bit of quiet, that's all.'

Holly kissed her granny, then lifted a hand in the general direction of Ron.

'I'll say goodnight, then. Granny will explain.'

She rose to her feet hurriedly because

she'd just caught a glimpse of Ben in the doorway.

A few paces behind him, beaming, stood the shameless, man-eating Julie, beaming.

Holly waited until she could see which side of the neighbouring table Ben was negotiating, before deliberately choosing the other way. Then, with a small wave and a smile as bright as she could muster, she edged towards the door, out of the bar . . . and out of his life.

* * *

Another beautiful day had dawned, and Granny Jean was already twittering with excitement at the thought of the morning to be spent in Honfleur, the last stop of the cruise.

'I'm so glad you're feeling better, Holly. Isn't it wonderful to be blessed with a strong constitution? I think you must get that from me. It would be nice if we had longer here, though,' she prattled on. 'I've heard the shopping's good, the town itself is very pretty and there's a park a short walk along the sea wall. There's also a couple of churches and, of course, the beautiful harbour. Come on, we need to hurry if we're to make the most of it — we've only got the morning, you know!'

Holly gave a grim smile. She really didn't feel like hurrying. Sharing a cabin with Granny Jean was, on occasions, rather similar to bunking with a small whirlwind!

But after a quick breakfast she found herself gathering together a street map of Honfleur, her camera and sunglasses plus, of course, one of her grandmother's panama hats. The hat was of the fold-up variety, and consequently had a rather wobbly brim, which made Holly feel like one of TV's Flowerpot Men. Although she desperately hoped she wouldn't bump into Ben while wearing it — though goodness knew why she should care any more what he thought — she knew she'd still be very grateful for its shade when the sun's heat increased.

Right, she could do this. It was the last day, and all she had to do if she saw him was smile, be polite and try and forget that kiss. A kiss which, it seemed, had been only one of many that he dropped around the place like so much confetti.

The guide books were correct. Honfleur, as well as being a working fishing port and popular yachting harbour, had also managed to preserve its artistic and rich historic heritage. Drinking in the picturesque, narrow cobbled streets, and eyeing the craft and gift shops and galleries that clustered all around, Granny Jean was beside herself with pleasure.

'To think a few months ago all this would have been a blur to me,' she said wonderingly. 'I'm so lucky!'

Then, more briskly, 'Shall we walk round the church and the old part of town first, then visit the shops? After that, if we have time, we can go to the park they mentioned.'

'Lovely,' Holly agreed, who hadn't been able to stop her bruised heart lifting a little at the sight of the colourful and typically French town waiting to be explored.

Just once Holly caught sight of Ben and Gramps. They were coming out of the wooden shingled church of St Catherine when she spotted them over by the bell tower. Quickly, and with a racing heart, she retraced her steps and hovered round a corner until they were out of sight.

'Goodness, I thought I'd lost you for a moment. Where did you disappear to?' Granny Jean asked when Holly caught up with her again. 'Although, this is such a small place, isn't it, that I couldn't really get lost. Even I could easily find my way back to the shuttle bus and then get on the right ship! Just look at that beautiful shop window. Come on, Holly, let's see if I can find something nice to spend my money on.'

Breathing a sigh of relief that she'd

managed to avoid Ben so easily, but still quite unnecessarily disturbed by the brief glimpse she'd had of him, Holly adjusted the unflattering panama hat and followed her grandmother into the maze of narrow streets with their invitingly quaint shops.

* * *

Two hours later found Ben sitting at a pavement café, with the remains of a cup of coffee in front of him. He was slightly surprised to find that Gramps was not already here at their pre-arranged meeting place, tapping impatiently with his stick and looking rather obviously at his watch.

Quite early on they'd arranged to split up — Gramps to go to the maritime museum situated inside Honfleur's oldest church, St Etienne, and Ben choosing instead to browse the harbour and shops.

He gave a crooked smile, because he'd also hoped that, in so doing, he might be lucky enough to bump into

Holly. He'd have enjoyed that.

Well, no such joy. He had not had even a small sighting of Holly, either at breakfast or here.

Or in the bar last night, come to that. In fact, Ben hadn't realised quite how much he'd wanted to see her until he'd had to spend the remainder of the evening listening to Granny Jean and Gramps reminiscing together about the war years.

It had been interesting, of course, but there was only so much talk about ration books and no bananas Ben could take at one time, thank you.

Still, when he did see her again — and he'd make sure he did — they could make up for lost time. Get to know one another.

Repeat that kiss, hopefully.

Not in its entirety, of course, along with the sun and the sea, the stillness and the very perfection of the moment. That would be impossible. But, for all that, the kiss had only been a starting point.

He scanned the crowds again. Still no sight of Gramps. He was fifteen minutes late now, probably lost in a world of maritime memorabilia. It was unusual for him not to be prompt. After all, he was the one who was always going on about the younger generation not recognising the vital importance of punctuality.

In the crowds, Ben caught sight of a girl with brown hair, wearing a lime green T-shirt that looked similar to one that Holly had worn the other day. Not too many girls could get away with that particular shade of green, he thought, even as he recognised with disappointment that the girl, though pretty enough, was not Holly.

A smile pulled at the corners of his mouth. Then his smile faded as he recalled that Holly had suddenly disappeared the night before because, according to Granny Jean, she'd felt queasy.

Still, she'd be feeling better this morning, surely.

Then he also remembered that she was considerably fairer-skinned than he was, and unlikely to be able to take so much sun. Although, the previous night she had looked wonderful, not in the least ill. Her skin had been glowing, her brown eyes sparkling.

Why had he ever had a moment of doubt that she was the girl for him? Because he had doubted, he admitted to himself. And after that kiss he'd been — face it, Ben — scared.

Scared of his feelings, scared of complications and of the future, if there was to be a future.

Just plain terrified. His life up until now had been fairly uncomplicated. His heart had managed to remain, at the same time as under going various infatuations, comparatively unbroken. No woman had affected him in the way that Holly had. He'd never felt the urge to, well, to settle down.

But then, after a day in St Peter Port without her, and then idiotically missing dinner because he'd fallen asleep, he had discovered something. When she'd walked into the theatre in her long cream dress, with her warm smile, he had found that, in fact, it really wasn't scary or complicated at all. He had realised that, probably, Holly was the best thing that had ever happened to him.

His brown-eyed girl. She had dominated the cruise for him.

Even when she was being so prickly, and he'd been trying so hard to impress her — with disastrous results, he admitted to himself with a smile. That should surely have given him a clue. He'd never bothered before.

He finished his cold coffee. He supposed he'd have to go and fish Gramps out of the museum. He'd obviously forgotten that they had to be back on board at one o'clock for the sailing at one thirty, and Ben would take great pleasure in mentioning the word 'punctual'.

* * *

Holly was close to panicking. It was twenty minutes to one and, over an hour ago, she'd lost Granny Jean.

At first she hadn't been seriously worried. Sooner or later they'd find each other, or meet up on their way to the dock. Granny Jean knew very well they had to be back on board at one o'clock.

The only trouble with her grandmother was her ability to completely underestimate the time factor, or appreciate that, however long it had taken to get to a certain point, it would take that same amount of time, if not longer, to return again.

Of course, she could be deep in conversation with someone she'd met in a shop or coffee bar, and probably be even now making her way to the shuttle with them.

But suppose she was on her own, had lost her bearings and couldn't find her way back to the shuttle bus?

Oh, Holly was being ridiculous. Granny Jean was bound to spot someone obviously English, and ask the way if she was lost.

Now time was getting on, and Holly had been up and down the narrow streets, and back to the shuttle collection point so many times she had lost count now.

She'd searched in the art galleries and the gift shops, and poked her head round the door of many of the boutiques. She had stared through the windows of the cafés and had stood by the harbour on the only route back to the shuttle.

Not a glimmer of Granny Jean.

What am I going to do? Holly thought. If not in a shop, where else would Granny Jean be? How on earth could she have been so careless as to lose her grandmother?

It wasn't like losing a pair of sunglasses, for goodness sake! Granny Jean had quite a presence. One moment she'd been there, gently fingering a dress that was far too young for her and which she'd had no intention of buying, simply enjoying the colours and touch of the fabric. The next moment, when Holly looked back in the shop, she'd vanished!

I should have stayed with her, Holly reproached herself. It was crazy to leave her alone even for a moment.

Holly was aware she'd been too wrapped up with her own problems; that was the trouble.

Too busy thinking about a certain tall, dark, charmer with light eyes and a devastating line in kisses. Now she stood alone on the harbour with her back to the maritime museum.

She felt like crying, and wished she'd never met Ben Brown.

'Hi, there!' a voice said behind her. 'I don't suppose you've seen Gramps, have you? He was supposed to meet me half an hour ago, and time's getting a bit tight.' Ben! Thank goodness!

Completely forgetting her earlier thoughts on the subject of Ben Brown, Holly now found herself nearly weeping with relief.

'I've lost Granny Jean, too! I've been looking for her for ages. She's not at the shuttle pick-up point, and the Anastasia won't wait, will it? We'll have to make our own way home, and I can't bear it. I just don't know what to do!' Her voice ended on a wobble and she gave a sniff.

'Okay, no need to panic. Might I say, by the by, what a singularly attractive hat you're wearing?'

Immediately Holly snatched the hat from her head.

'No, you may not! I don't know how you can be so cool about it.'

'Well, it is a pretty cool hat.'

'Not the hat! Granny Jean — and Ron, too,' she added as an afterthought.

'Well, the fact that they're both missing makes me feel better. I reckon they're together, and have gone walkabout. It's not one o'clock yet, and the ship doesn't sail till one thirty. So there's still time.'

'But I've been everywhere! I can't think where else she'd have gone.'

'I've just looked in the maritime

museum, because that was the last place Gramps was speaking about visiting. He definitely wasn't there, but I don't believe for a moment that he's lost. You could dump Gramps in the middle of the Sahara and he'd still find his way home. He's got an in-built compass in his brain!'

'Granny Jean hasn't,' Holly said despondently.

Ben took a map from the back pocket of his shorts.

'Now, where else would they have gone?' He studied the town map for a moment, taking his finger to the north. 'Ah, we did discuss maybe taking the walk along the sea wall to the new park — the Garden of Fame. I wonder if that's what he's done.'

'Granny Jean mentioned the park as well. But then she seemed to go off the idea, saying she didn't think we had time to do both.' Holly frowned. 'No, I really don't think she'd have done that on her own.'

'I bet she would have if she'd met up

with someone else who was wanting to doit.'

Ben's light-eyed gaze stared into her, and in spite of everything Holly's heart skipped a treacherous beat.

'What do you think? Shall we head for the park?'

It was such a relief to have someone to share a worry with.

'You don't think we should split up, maybe?'

'No.' Ben spoke firmly. 'You've already looked round them. If I find that pair, I'd then have to come back again and find you! Anyway, heaven forbid, but if anything has happened to one of them we'd need two of us — one to go for help, and one to stay at the scene.'

Holly's eyes widened with horror as she took in the import of his words.

'You don't really think something bad has happened, do you?'

He gave a grin.

'No, of course not. But I am aware it's extremely unusual for Gramps to be late for his lunch ever since we've been on this cruise. He loves it.'

As they'd been speaking Ben had gradually been ushering her towards the sea wall path. Trying to keep up with his long stride, Holly hurried along beside him.

She felt better now she was walking.

'Honestly, when I find Granny I'm going to be so cross!'

'Yep, me too. This is the second time Gramps has had me chasing after him,' Ben said grimly. 'Last time was in the middle of the night. I thought he'd fallen overboard. What on earth I'd have told my mother I don't know!'

'They're a responsibility, aren't they? Grandparents?'

'I'll say,' he agreed. 'I don't suppose Granny Jean has a mobile phone, does she?'

'She does, but it's in the cabin safe.'

'Gramps hasn't even got one. Considers them unnecessary. Maybe he'll change his mind after this . . . Here, steady!'

His arm shot out, and he caught Holly's arm as she stumbled against a kerb. Suddenly they were standing very close. Too close.

For a moment, Holly remained motionless, only aware of Ben and the magic he seemed able to produce just with his touch, that was pulsating all around her.

'Sorry, I'm going too fast for you.'

'No, you're not.'

Holly struggled to remember that this man was nothing but a serial kisser and an outrageous flirt. That he no doubt looked at every pretty girl in exactly the way he was looking at her now, as though there were only the two of them in the world.

'It's my own stupid fault for not looking where I'm going.'

Gently, Ben slackened his hold on her arm, but held her gaze, the concern naked in his eyes.

'I'd forgotten for a moment; you weren't well yesterday, were you?'

'Um, er, I'm better today, thanks. But

I thought a hat would be wise . . . Never mind about that. We have to find them. I'm getting seriously worried.' With a supreme effort of will, she jerked away from his eyes and looked back at the road ahead.

'Oh, thank goodness!'

There, in the distance, the tall, thin frame of Gramps had come into view. Limping painfully, but making slow but sure progress by leaning heavily on Gramps's stick on one side and his arm on the other, was her small, silver-haired grandmother.

A feeling of relief washed over Holly and she broke into a run.

10

Where on earth have you been?' Holly almost shouted as soon as she judged the errant pair to be in earshot.

'First things first, young lady,' Ron interrupted, still ushering Granny Jean along gently. 'One of you had better get to the shuttle bus and ask them to wait for us — Jean isn't up to rushing.'

'I'll go,' Ben offered, glancing at his watch. 'We should still be in time.'

He set off at a sprint.

Holly took in the pallor of her grandmother's determinedly smiling, though pained, face.

'Sorry, Granny. I didn't mean to scream at you, but I've been so worried! It's not like you to go gallivanting off on your own.'

'I wasn't gallivanting anywhere! When I couldn't find you, well, I thought I'd walk just a little way along towards the park and see how much time there was.' She shrugged. 'But then I turned my ankle stepping on a loose bit of paving. The pain just got worse, so I took my shoe off. I couldn't get my shoe on again, so I had to sort of hop around a bit.'

'Jean,' Ron spoke firmly. 'Save the dramatics for later. We have to get you to the shuttle. Now, concentrate.'

'Yes, Ron,' Granny Jean replied meekly.

Holly was left standing open-mouthed at this surprising submission from her usually feisty grandmother.

'Darling, don't be difficult.'

Granny Jean had just been seen by the ship's doctor, who had pronounced the ankle strained but not seriously damaged, and she was resting in the cabin.

'I've told you I'm fine now, and if I rest up for a couple of hours watching a film or something, I'll be able to come down for dinner.

'Now, be a good girl, and go and join in the quiz with Ben and Ron.'

For a moment, as she left the cabin, Holly thought that it might be possible, after all, for her to do as her grandmother had suggested. Hadn't she spoken to Ben this morning easily enough? They had joined forces and found Granny Jean and Ron successfully. It hadn't been so hard.

That was because you were worried about Granny Jean missing the boat, said a small voice inside her head. There was no choice in the matter. And anyway, be truthful with yourself — you nearly fainted like a soppy, Victorian heroine when he touched you!

Then again, whispered another voice, after tomorrow you'll never see him again in your lifetime.

Holly put a hand to her burning cheek, then resolutely squared her shoulders. At the quiz Ron would be there as a buffer between them. All she needed to do was be polite; that, and not let Ben Brown come within touching distance.

She took a deep breath before

pushing open the swing doors.

Ben and Ron were in the act of seating themselves. Blonde, man-eating Julie was standing alongside them. Well, alongside Ben, actually, laughing and tilting her head back in a way that made Holly want to scratch her eyes out. Ben, nevertheless, seemed to be listening with rapt attention to whatever it was Julie was saying.

Without stepping inside, Holly let the swing door shut.

She didn't want to go to the rotten old quiz anyway. She'd much rather take a stroll round the deck.

Yes, this was much better. Who wanted to be cooped up inside when there was all this lovely fresh air out here, just waiting to be breathed in and out? So bracing.

And if, maybe the sea breeze caught your eyes and made them water, well, it was easy to just dash the tears away with the back of your hand. Wasn't it?

Holly collected a cup of tea and found herself a seat in the sun, away from everyone else. She sat watching the waves.

Tomorrow morning they'd be back at Harwich. Great, she could get on with her life. The cruise had been great. The people she'd met had been great. The whole thing had been great.

Why then, did she feel so totally, utterly, miserable?

* * *

Ben's eyes were continually straying towards the door. Where was Holly? Surely she knew they both had things to talk about? Tomorrow morning they would be back at Harwich, and he didn't even possess her phone number.

Tonight at dinner and then the show, which Gramps and Granny Jean would be bound to want to watch — well, there'd be no privacy. And then, suppose she didn't want to come to the Imperial bar afterwards? Suppose she had to do last minute packing or something?

'Now, here's one for Ben Brown, I think.'

It was a smiling, winking, Julie who was running the quiz today, speaking sexily into the microphone and staring across the room directly at Ben.

Ben gave a restrained smile.

'From which country did Don Juan originate?'

Oh, ha ha, very funny, Ben thought. He'd just about had enough of this. He looked around. Gramps was happily conferring with Tony the ex-policeman and his wife Linda as to the answer.

'Catch you later, Gramps,' he said into the old man's ear. 'I'm going to get some air.'

Once on deck, he felt better. Not good, but better. Part of him still felt irrationally cross with Gramps for looking quite so smug when he'd imparted the news that he'd decided the time had come for him to get out a bit more. He also informed an astonished Ben that he fully intended to keep up his friendship with Granny Jean.

'It's only a friendship mind,' he'd insisted. 'She talks a lot of sense. Not all the time, of course! But it can't hurt for me to join a few clubs, that sort of thing — and it always helps if you know someone already.'

Smiling to himself Ben leaned on the ship's rail for a while, just looking at the translucency of the waves and trying to ignore a sharp knot of anxiety making itself felt in the vicinity of his heart.

It would be okay. Of course it would. Holly wasn't avoiding him, not really. She was probably doing her packing now, but at dinner they might get a chance to talk together.

He'd make sure they got that chance to talk together. They could skip the show, leave Gramps and Jean, happily enjoying music from the shows, and sneak off somewhere and have a chat.

Together, the two of them — with no bystanders.

Ben turned, and made his way to the aft of the ship and the lower deck where there always seemed to be a cup of tea going.

Then his heart gave a lurch. Away

from everyone else, a slight figure with chestnut brown hair sat hunched over a mug. With a frowning intensity she was staring at the sea as though nothing else mattered.

'I'm beginning to think you're avoiding me.' He placed his mug of tea squarely next to hers and took a chair opposite.

Eventually Holly looked up.

'I'm not avoiding you,' she said levelly. 'I just didn't fancy the quiz. I was enjoying my own company,' she added pointedly.

Ben cleared his throat.

This wasn't going to plan. It seemed Holly had built up the wall again; that impenetrable wall of polite indifference. But she wasn't indifferent; he knew better.

'I was wondering . . .' he started hesitantly. 'I was wondering if we could maybe meet up in Colchester? When we get back home, I mean.'

She picked up her mug and took a sip of tea.

'Why would we want to do that?'

This wasn't getting any easier. He tried to give a casual shrug to his shoulders, with limited success.

'Why not? We could just meet up a couple of times, see what comes of it, couldn't we? We seem to get on well, I can't believe we haven't met up before. After all, we both work in Colchester.'

Holly gave a sound which was very nearly a sigh.

'Ben, we're very different kinds of people.'

'What's that supposed to mean?'

There was silence.

He tried again.

'How do you arrive at that conclusion exactly? Different how? Two heads? What . . . ?'

He looked away, trying to hide the hurt in his heart.

'I thought you liked me, Holly. Look, I know we didn't get off to a good start, and that was my fault, I admit it. It was because . . . '

Careful, Ben, he warned himself.

You're beginning to sound desperate, and desperate is hardly attractive.

'Look,' he began again, more quietly this time. 'I'm sorry if I behaved like a bit of a prat at first. But, well, I think I knew even then how much I could learn to like you and, if I'm honest, this trip was supposed to be a writing trip for me. And what have I produced? About four pages of complete rubbish.'

Holly's eyes remained fixed on the sea.

Suddenly he clapped his hand to his head. What a fool he'd been!

'I know you denied it before, but there is a boyfriend, isn't there?'

Ah, that had elicited a response. She glanced at him quickly and seemed to debate her answer.

'Not any more, there isn't. No, we broke up quite recently, well, six months ago. I'm happy on my own. Single.'

No boyfriend then? He smiled with relief.

'So am I. Yep, Happy to be single.

Certainly I am. But it would be nice to meet up. You know, just meet up?'

There was another long pause. Then she looked directly at him.

'I don't do casual lovemaking.'

He blinked. Well, that was unexpectedly direct.

'Neither do I,' he replied once he'd got over the shock.

A smile creased the corners of his eyes.

'I always insist on full evening dress.'

Not funny, Ben! he reproved himself. Too flippant. He held his breath.

Suddenly, just as he thought he'd really blown it and there was no way back, the corner of her mouth twitched, and a chuckle escaped her.

'I was trying to be serious!'

'I know. So was I, believe it or not. Didn't seem to work, though, did it?'

Holly smoothed her unused paper napkin.

'Look, Ben, you're a laugh, I'll admit it, and it's been fun. But I don't play games. I don't flirt with all and sundry.'

He felt his eyes narrow.

'Well, I do do friendly. But no, on the whole, I don't play games either. At least, I don't think I do, not when it comes to other people's feelings, anyway. Is there a point to this?'

'Well, you could have fooled me.'

She looked away, cross at having blurted out her pain.

'Hang on, I don't understand.'

She shrugged.

'There's nothing to understand. As I said, we're different people. I don't need to meet up with you in Colchester to realise that. And it's no good giving me that innocent look! I saw you! I saw you with Julie out on deck. I didn't disturb what was obviously a romantic moment made for two . . . ' Her voice petered out on a wobble.

'You wouldn't have noticed me anyway,' she went on in a stronger tone. 'You were locked together in the moonlight. When was it now? The day after Tresco, I believe?

'I thought Tresco meant something to

you. But obviously not, because in my book you don't do that. You don't go off into a clinch with someone else. Not after Tresco. Not after you've kissed someone with your very heart and soul, as though you meant it . . . '

There was no use trying to stay calm. She was shaking now.

'So, you see? There you are, I was right. You're very nice, Ben Brown. Good for a laugh. But we're different people.'

She glanced at her watch.

'Now, if you'll excuse me, I'm going to check on Granny Jean . . . '

Screwing up the paper napkin she'd spent so long in smoothing out, and picking up her cup in one fluid movement, she turned away without looking at him.

'See you at dinner.'

And Ben was left staring after her, an expression of complete bewilderment on his face.

On the whole, Holly thought, she'd handled that rather well. There had been a moment when she'd thought she might disgrace herself and cry, certainly. But she'd managed to express herself perfectly eloquently.

She felt triumphant as she walked along the deck to her own cabin.

Yes, she'd done it! She'd put Ben Brown in his place.

The euphoria didn't last very long, however. No matter how often she congratulated herself on finding out just how fickle Ben was, thereby saving herself a lot of heartache in the future, the memory kept coming back. The memory of how he made her laugh, how he made her heart beat faster just by being near her. It haunted her thoughts.

But she had little time to brood. Much recovered after her rest, Granny Jean was now clearly annoyed with herself for twisting her ankle. With the aid of Ron's stick, however, she was determined to appear at dinner.

'I must thank Ron properly. He was very kind, very kind indeed. I'm not sure I deserved it. He sat with me until the worst of the pain went off, then insisted that I used his stick. Quite a gentleman!'

'More than can be said for his grandson,' Holly muttered.

'Didn't catch that, darling?'

Holly busied herself in rolling up T-shirts.

'Nothing. How will Ron manage without his stick?'

'He'll survive. If you ask me, he only brought it as protection. He wanted to be able to plead an aching leg if he didn't want to do something!

'Now.' She put her head on one side. 'What's with you two love birds?'

'Pardon me?'

'You and Ben.'

Holly gave a hollow laugh.

'Oh, please. Love birds?'

Her grandmother looked disappointed. 'Now, don't tell me I'm wrong.'

'You are wrong.'

'He's very keen on you, you know. And you like him now — I can see that.

Come on, you can tell me. Are you going to get together in Colchester?'

Holly gave an exasperated sigh.

'No, we are not. We've only known each other for a few days. Which, I might add, was more than adequate, thanks!'

'No need to bite my head off, dear. It just seemed so romantic, that's all. You looked so right together, from the start. I thought you were falling in love. Oh, well, my mistake, I suppose.'

'Yes it was. Love is not in the equation.'

'Love is all around, Holly,' Granny Jean corrected her. 'If you'd just open your eyes and see it.'

Dinner was a quiet affair. After a hot morning in Honfleur and a sunny afternoon at sea, all the passengers looked contented but drowsy.

Moodily, Holly picked at her food. To her right she half attended to a conversation taking place between Ron and her grandmother. It sounded as though he was agreeing that he would come to her club's next gardening lecture, and possibly even join a club that arranged outings to the theatre.

She sighed. Who would have thought that the older generation, fixed in their ways as they were meant to be, were so easily able to bury their differences, while younger people avoided all eye contact?

At last, the meal was over, and they headed in the direction of the show. Noticing Ron's over-solicitous concern about Granny Jean's walking ability, Holly hid a smile as she followed behind.

'It's a lovely evening,' Ben said in her ear. 'Why don't we go outside? I'd like to talk to you.'

'You already did,' she replied coldly. 'There's nothing to add.'

He didn't answer, but the expression on his face was steely as he opened the swing doors for Ron and Granny Jean to pass through. Holly made as though to follow, but was stopped by his hand gripping her elbow firmly.

'We have unfinished business, Holly,' he said roughly. 'You had your say, and you walked away from me without giving me a chance to reply. That's unfair, and you know it.'

Aware that her heart was racing in a way it had no business to, Holly tried to look dignified at the same time as avoiding his gaze.

'All right, I'll listen. But you'll have to make it quick.'

This time she didn't object as he pulled her through the doors to the deck. Outside, the darkening sky was streaked with pink.

Ben leaned on the rail and Holly stood beside him, watching the grey-green waves, with their foamy frilled edges, divide as the Anastasia sedately powered through them.

'I need to explain.'

Ben sounded nervous. He wasn't looking at her, it was almost as though he was addressing the sea. He took a deep breath.

'Holly, I really want to see you again.

It might not work out — I don't know. But surely we should give it a try?'

If only she could believe him! She wanted to, with all her heart.

But how could she, with that picture of him and Julie locked together in a passionate embrace playing over and over again in her memory?

He turned to face her, his blue eyes burning in his tanned face.

'Tresco did mean something to me. To tell the truth, it put me into a state of shock! Gave me a jolt. I didn't know I could feel like that. I didn't want to feel like that . . . about anyone.

'But I did, and I do. It's like getting chickenpox. Only, unlike chickenpox — it doesn't go away.'

Something stirred in Holly's heart. He looked sincere. He sounded absolutely sincere.

But again, how could she trust him after what she had witnessed?

'The Julie thing,' he went on. 'I thought you knew that was all one-sided. Oh, Lord, this is going to sound big-headed. But I've been trying to avoid that woman ever since we came on board! Ask Gramps, he thinks it's highly amusing, even if I don't!

'Yesterday, after dinner, I thought I'd just slip out on deck for a moment to cool down. I leaned on the rail of the ship, just like we're doing now. I was watching the waves and thinking about you. The next thing I knew Julie was there next to me. She took me unawares. Next thing I knew, she'd pulled my head down and was giving me a passionate kiss . . . Yuk!'

Her heart was beating loudly in her ears. Dare she believe he was telling the truth?

'Against all my usual instincts, I caught her by the shoulders and forced her away from me. I told her I was sorry but, tempting though she was, my feelings were already engaged elsewhere.'

Holly said nothing. The moment stretched into a full minute.

'Well, it's up to you,' he said at

length. 'I've told you the truth. If you don't trust me, then there's no hope for us and, well, I guess I agree, no point in meeting again.'

The last rays of the sun were glinting in Ben's hair as Holly slowly turned towards him. For a long moment she let her eyes stare into his.

His expression was hopeful but strangely vulnerable. The confident, cocky Ben was nowhere in sight.

'I do believe you,' she said at last.

Then after another moment when she didn't know whether to laugh or cry, she began to speak.

'For the whole of this trip I've been scared. Scared of liking you too much, scared of letting my feelings show. I don't know why you even like me, I've been so, so horrible. I'm sorry. I couldn't really believe you liked me enough to — well . . . '

Tears sparkled on the ends of her lashes as she looked up at him.

'To fall in love with you?' he asked softly.

The sun was very low in the sky now. He gave a smile that turned into a groan. He took a step towards her.

'Oh, my brown eyed girl,' he said.

With a last glimmer of golden light the sun sank beneath the horizon.

'Oh, my brown eyed girl.'

THE END

Other titles in the
Linford Romance Library:

TERESA'S TREASURE

Valerie Holmes

Teresa, as a child, dreamt of the day when the secret inside a tin box would be revealed to her. However, as she grows into a young woman her life charges dramatically, shattering her childhood dreams . . . yet she still remembers her treasure. Risking a possible marriage match, Teresa decides to go on a journey of discovery to seek it out. But some secrets are meant to stay buried. What she discovers is of greater value than she had ever imagined.

THE SHOWMAN'S GIRL

Julia Douglas

When Emily runs away with the circus in the 1930s, she enters a magical world of perilous adventures, intense friendships and deep passions. Growing up in the big top, she admires, from afar, the charismatic showman, Adam Strand. But Adam is torn between his wife Jayne, a daredevil tight-wire walker, and Molly, the elephant trainer who's always carried a torch for him. Emily becomes a star — but will she ever be able to tell Adam how she really feels?

A PERFECT ARRANGEMENT

Kay Gregory

'*You'd suit me very well. You're tidy, you're intelligent, you're unlikely to vamp me . . . And you can type!*' Hardly the most flattering description Holly had ever heard — but for all Ethan Yorke's arrogance — his job offer *was* tempting. And plain Holly, in her business suits and glasses, knew that she was safe . . . Ethan would never look twice at her! So why did she have to go and do a foolish thing like falling in love with him?

DARE TO LOVE

Chrissie Loveday

Back in 1930, when Nellie marries James, the owner of a pottery factory, her future looks wonderful. However, moving into a different social class brings its issues. She is now the mistress of the house, where once she was a lowly maidservant, and, despite being able to help her family financially, they have their own problems in life and she can never resist interfering. But with her strength of character and talents, she will usually win the day . . .